Ages of Entanglement

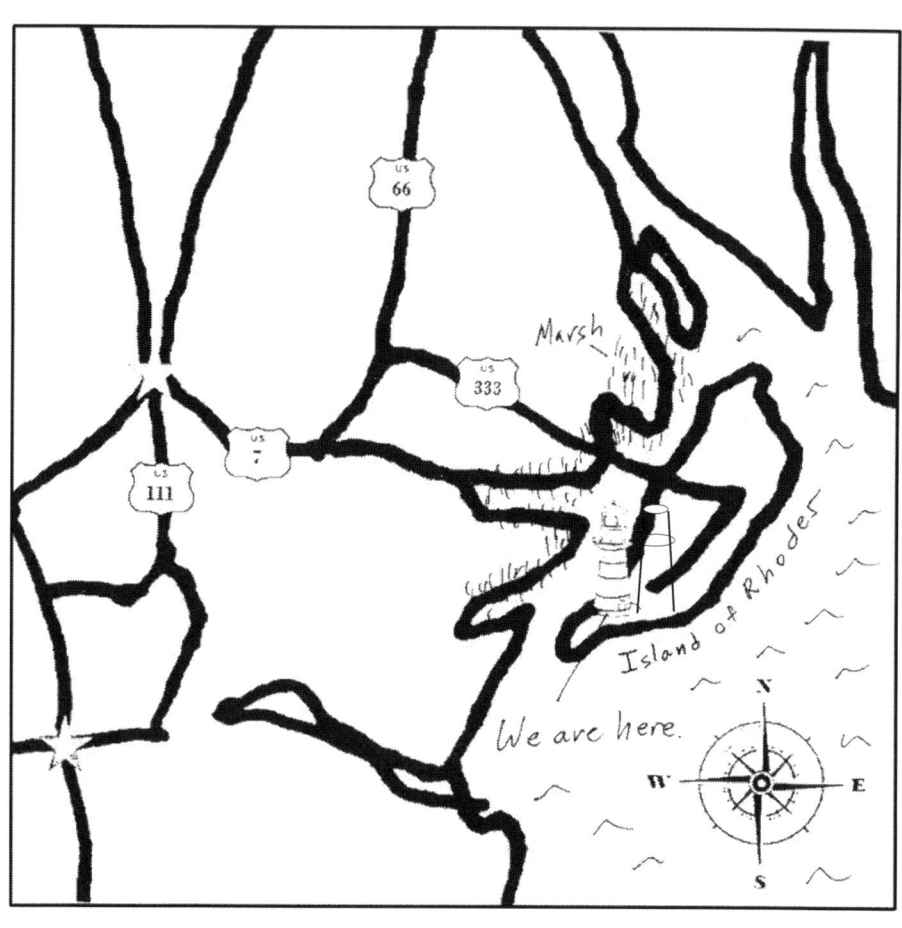

Ages of Entanglement
Robert L. Jackson

Humid Tea and Dry Pines Publishing
2019

Copyright © 2019 by Robert L. Jackson III

All rights reserved. This book or any portion thereof may not be reproduced or used in any manner whatsoever without the express written permission of the publisher except for the use of brief quotations in a book review or scholarly journal.

First Printing: 2019

ISBN 978-0-359-96269-3

Humid Tea and Dry Pines Publishing

www.rjackson.onuniverse.com

www.eng.auburn.edu/~jacksr7/Interests.htm

Ordering Information:

Special discounts are available on quantity purchases by corporations, associations, educators, and others. For details, contact the publisher at the above listed address.

U.S. trade bookstores and wholesalers: Please contact Humid Tea and Dry Pines Publishing, email: rljackson3@gmail.com

Dedication

To all whom share this universe, and to those I am entangled with, especially my children.

Acknowledgement

Thank you to those who helped refine this work and encouraged me along the way. This includes all the teachers in our lives.

Chapter 1: Awaken

The crackling heat of smoldering wood radiated the young man's skin. The sound of metal crying as it collapsed under its own weight filled the air around him. No voices, or sounds of agony, rose from the wreckage. His beaten body lay limp on the forest floor, but the healing energy of youth already filled his arteries. Suddenly, his body and mind aged, because this was merely a memory resurfacing from three decades ago. The nightmare ended.

The old man's eyes cracked open the brittle frost sealing his lashes. The sun attempted to overcome the obstructions of clouds, mountains, and trees, as it had always done for all of humankind. His breath floated up as vapor from a warm spring. It was time to go south.

Through the years, the irises of his eyes had seemingly bleached from an ocean blue to that of salty foam under the constant barrage of ultra violet waves (the ones you can't see but do the most damage). Just as the choppy ocean conceals the jagged coral, his eyes floated above a lethal reef that lie protecting the contents of his soul.

During this age, upon this sparsely traveled ocean of a lost country, the reef protected a sacred harbor inside him, that he let no one access. It could be a refuge of last resort, but now he hardly remembered it was there. Many aggressive and empty vessels of people had fallen to this barrier, and it kept him alive. But some individuals, empty soulless vessels, without luggage or cargo, float high in the water and can slip across hidden barriers just below the surface. Maybe that's why many that he had met in the current age strove to empty themselves.

Despite the haze of his aging eyes, he could still see well enough to get by, although the world now seemed less sharp and through a foggy lens. Perhaps this was not critically important, because it was a world with less boundaries to filter lives.

No place existed now to get your vision tested for and to buy new glasses. Sometimes he would keep an old pair of reading glasses, but he didn't read much anymore. He also used to wear sunglasses, but they inevitably were scratched, broken or lost. It really didn't matter anymore, so he stopped worrying about that as well.

The hairs shot from his head like the white trails from rockets trying to escape the gravity of his dense mind. They sometimes succeeded in breaking free and took with them facts and memories to alien worlds. Would we ever cross the horizon and reunite with those memories, those settlers of time and space? Sometimes they brought with them the weights of our mind, freeing us to expand, and replant old fields with new crops. But some recollections of pure love and acceptance were lost, and it seemed that he was destined to never sit at those dinner tables with family again. But did a meal, or a voice, exist if it was forgotten? He realized that some things were gone and he did his best to anchor down those memories he deemed important in tethers of repetition. In sleep, some would still lift off in dreams and orbit until they tumbled into the cosmos.

Other white hair flowed from around his mouth and chin into a ragged beard. It resembled the foam gathering around the bow of a ship cutting through the sea.

How could one choose which vessels to anchor and protect from the impending storm of age, and which ones to allow to set sail on the endlessness of outer space? It was a difficult decision, but he automatically made some selections based on the direst of his needs. He had to survive in a world where the social constructs and technological support systems were in ruins.

"From rockets to ruins," he often thought. Although rockets had not brought the ruins, the rocket age was still gone and mankind had lost the means to push to another frontier. In these ruins he repeated the chosen actions daily, weekly and monthly that were needed to survive. He would start by rekindling his campfire that had consumed itself in the night to boil some water. It was much easier to rekindle a fire than to start a new one. That, however, never kept him from leaving the old ones. From a little dry kindling of small sticks, the smoke would first grow and then the flames would catch again.

In a battered but lightweight aluminum pot he would pour some of the water he had collected over the past few days from creeks and water trickling from mountain rocks. Water in the mountains was typically cleaner and safer than in lower, warmer areas. Nonetheless, it usually was a good idea to sterilize it unless it came directly from rain, snow, or a cold spring.

On a prosperous day he would mix in some coffee powder, but usually he would mix in some leaves he had stuffed away. Hibiscus made a reasonable tea and could be found in warmer climates. Yaupin, which had been gaining popularity before the Fall of civilization, was the best option. Yaupin is an evergreen, so in the winter he would keep an eye out for it. The plant grew in scattered locations around the Southeast and he tried to keep track of good colonies. Apparently Yaupin was the only indigenous plant with caffeine, and that made it valuable. When he did see another traveler, he could also trade it.

Sassafras could also be found and used to make something that resembled root beer, at least in smell. It also worked well as a blood coagulant, which was important for him. His blood didn't always clot so well, which could be dangerous when penetrating the overgrowth. Sassafras had been banned in civilized times because of a link to cancer. No one was here now to govern and he figured, "why the hell not."

Periodically he would find old farms that had other non-native, but useful plants. He noticed that over the years they had diminished; probably because they just weren't a good fit for the soil, parasites, and climate. Man had used his energy to force them to flourish.

Sometimes the reverse would happen, and non-native species would thrive and grow without bounds. Kudzu was a good example of this. It had taken over the landscapes of warmer areas, and even now continued to spread and dominate. However, even the aggressive kudzu grows an exquisitely beautiful flower behind its flowing green mass. Periodically, he would scrounge through the brush to find one. For some reason it gave him hope. The flower below the rolling green was like a coral reef hidden below the ocean's surface. The hidden flower reminded him that maybe something valuable still existed in this fallen world.

After boiling water, he would eat. His diet varied drastically. Could be bird one day, squirrel the next, and fish a week later. Fish were relatively easy to catch when near a larger body of water. He found it humorous how fish had turned from a commoner's food to a delicacy as man prospered. Even lobsters were once considered 'bugs' and fed to the prisoners in Maine. Now all these social structures had crumbled. The once united and yet divided states really could not be discerned now either, except by the rusted signs on some once important roads.

Today, several twisted apples were on the menu. They were ripening before the onset of winter. This area of the Smoky Mountains had once been known for them. There would be no apple festival this year, or in the foreseeable future, but maybe one day someone would revive it, or more likely, reinvent it. A good apple cider would definitely make any day extraordinary.

Did he ever miss the refined menu of civilization? Not too much. That modern diet had degraded human biology and his own, but now he had recovered. It seemed that biologically humans were not meant to eat the mass produced diet of geometric shapes. Many people had known it, but to change meant giving up convenience and low cost. Unless he ate something questionable, such as certain berries and plants, or uncooked and rancid meat, his body ran smooth. This is how our biology had evolved to eat, he thought.

After eating, his body responded to the nutrition with a sudden burst of energy. His mind responded as well. It was time to go south, but he only knew that from the changing temperatures and foliage. To anyone observing him, he was always lost, or wandering, but how could one be considered lost without having a specified destination? He remembered having destinations and goals in the past, but time had disintegrated all maps, and all that remained was the guidance of biology. He had spent years searching for all the connections he had to his original life. He found none of them.

The only chains he had not broken, were that of the weather. But like migrating herds, it coerced him into traveling in a more or less consistent direction. Somehow, he actually felt freer now than before. Maybe he had forgotten how to miss things, and people. The shackles of society were always rusting, but they had finally broken from him in a brittle failure. He was now free of society.

Now the sun glowed, fully unrefined by any branches or leaves. The heat felt good on his cold bones. He gathered the aluminum pot, foam ground covering and the few things he had back into an old canvas pack. He tightened straps around a weathered and repaired sleeping bag. He had stitched tough leather and canvas over the tattered edges and gaping tears of the bag with large gruesome stitches. He would waterproof the leather and other items, such as his shoes, with oil. Usually the oil came from meat he had cooked. The sleeping bag proved even more reliable and durable than before, but a bit heavier.

The handmade laces of his boots tightened the leather around his feet. His boots and shoes wore out fast. The machine woven laces had long ago frayed and broke. Cut and stretched animal skin and internal membranes worked well as replacements. The soles would also wear. Old tire rubber and other similar materials often lasted longer than the soft rubber and foam of the original shoes. Soft things typically wore out much more quickly than hard things. This also was true of people living in this time.

He picked up a tall stick, sharpened on one end. It was not a thick heavy stick, but narrow. Its thickness still made it strong enough to provide some support while walking. He had this particular stick for only a few weeks. He would whittle new sticks periodically, and use the old ones for firewood.

The sun was slowly rising to his left as he headed toward an opening in the brush ahead of him. This lead to a natural path, and only a few branches of leaves had to be pushed aside. Eventually, the dense foliage opened to a pine forest canopy. The land rose and fell in gentle waves ahead. Pine needles covered the ground in an impervious crosshatching. The shade and the fallen leaves helped to keep the smaller and newer plants from growing. The openness came with a cost however, as the needles made the sloped earth slippery. The sharp walking stick helped him to stabilize himself from time to time.

With careful steps he followed the side of a ridge amid the silent trees. The ridge slowly disappeared and the land lowered into a stony stream bed. The water was clear and looked cool. There might be enough water for trout, and although he would eventually need food, he currently desired to continue on his path. A fallen trunk served as a bridge across the stream. It creaked as its rotting fibers strained under his steps. Across the stream the land rose, and continued to rise toward a peak, out of view, but existing beyond the trees. He began to walk straight up the slope until it grew too steep to traverse directly. Then he zigzagged at a pleasant angle and slowly rose.

The density of trees dissipated and large boulders protruded from the ribs of the mountain. The sky now revealed itself in an autumn blue. The sun–following its path toward the opposite horizon–had reached the midway point. The source of light had risen well above the foliage, and yet the air still felt a bit too cool. Perhaps winter was rearing its head from above the humid blur of summer.

His precise steps continued upward toward the peak. The rock faces became more prolific, and the trees became scarce. Those that rooted were of the perseverant kind. From bare roots clinging to the stone, their twisted branches flowed upward to find light. The sun stood without rival now. Yet, he sensed something moving stealthily above. His eyesight began to appear hazy. The shadows emitted curved fangs along their edges, the result of succumbing to quantum physics. He had seen this before.

These images marked the coming of a solar eclipse. He did not know if it was a total eclipse, and if the moon would reach cosmic perfection, aligning its edges with those of the more distant sun. The sun was a relentless foe. Helios degraded every bit of evolution with its beams. Eyes saw in blurred images. Hair lightened, and grew weaker. Flesh and skin absorbed the energy and degraded forever at a genetic level.

This reminded him of Florida. Its coasts, fully consumed by man, and all areas under the constant attack of the sun. Everything seemed to become pale and bleached. They called the colors pastel. But truly, they were just primary colors defeated in battle. Chemical bonds were no match for the phonons. They were recognized by Einstein as the only thing capable of the ultimate speed, and therefore the limiting energy. Nothing could ever match light on the battlefield of physics, except a shadow...and a black hole.

As he walked past stones, governed by a different timescale, the sun continued to dim. It seemed that the lunar goddess had seduced the sun or gained his favor, and slowly dimmed his power. Sunset should be several hours away, and yet nature began to recognize her outgoing tide of light. The insects began to chirp and sing for their mates.

Suddenly, the sky went nearly black, and he paused his strides. Above, the fabric of the sun's robe twirled and oscillated around the black silhouette of the conquering moon. The distant stars and galaxies appeared, and mapped the universe. This was the beauty in the world, amplified by the intercourse of interstellar beings.

In the distance, he thought he heard the sound of a group, or maybe a village, exclaim at the event. It did not sound like screams of terror, but rather like celebration, perhaps of an alignment with the expected arrival of mythical forces.

He wondered if somewhere in the world people lived who could not recognize the eclipse's celestial meaning. To one unaware of celestial mechanics it would seem as if the world were ending, and then having this demise disappear after just a few minutes. Those beings, freed of science, might decipher it as a warning, or a reminder, of what loomed outside the primitive, but predictable, cycles.

Something percolated through his mind. Words formed from images and mechanisms. He used to write these down, but with no likelihood of them ever being read, he had stopped. Now they only formed, and then dissolved in his mind. Perhaps they did not dissolve, but travelled to another realm where they forever engraved on some eternal form of matter.

The words became solid as he repeated them and filled in the gaps. The looping process of his mind converged on:

The lunar shadow,
traverses the light
with the elegance
of a black dress.
When she covers
the reactor,
the sheath
reveals the barrier reef
around the sun.
Succinct darkness
affects green ideas little,
but plants
eggs in the mind
that grow in prophecy
to cause misdirection
and degradation.

Chapter 2: Shadows

After the sun returned, he continued his motion, but the sickle shaped shadows remained for some time. From the peak he began his descent down toward thicker woodlands. The pines, ancient beings, grew taller once again. The leaves filtered more and more of the light and less foliage blocked his path.

He wondered who had witnessed the sun's temporary defeat. Amid the echoes of the mountains, he found it difficult to determine which direction the voices had come from. Unless he knew a group of people, he would usually try to stay clear of them. This practice was not just for safety, but he was not fully conscience of the true reason. He had reached freedom from any social structure, and any interaction with a group could result in entanglement.

Entanglement. In quantum physics, entanglement was strange but undeniable. In space, a particle floated freely, only interacting at a safe distance with surrounding populations, and following a path that would appear random to us. But then someone realized the immense quantum power between particles—forever intertwining them together by an infinitely strong and instantaneously reactive thread. This quantum entanglement occurred simply by the act of observing one of the particles. By controlling the observations, one could entangle particles forever, and then control one with the other. He feared this attachment.

Samson, in his original vocation, would explain to customers the concept of quantum entanglement by using the primitive example of Schrodinger's cat. It goes like this. First consider a cat that is placed in a box with a lethal mechanism that kills the cat exactly half of the time. In quantum mechanics, the cat is considered both alive and dead until the box is opened, and the cat is observed. Now consider two cats with two of the identical box devices. The cats are placed in the boxes simultaneously. If the cats are entangled via quantum mechanics, then a strange thing occurs. Quantum entanglement dictates that if the box is opened and that cat is alive, than the other will always be dead, and vice versa. The cats are never both alive or both dead. They are forever linked and controlled by quantum entanglement. By killing—or protecting—one cat, one could control the fate of the other cat. In the same way one could control entangled matter.

Leaning against a large pine to rest, one of his few remaining memories resurfaced. He recalled standing on a flat terrain echoing out as far as the eyes could see. The ground was dry, and a steady wind stirred up swirls of dusty soil. The only noticeable features on the land were a road that had brought him here, a sleek black vehicle behind him, and several dry irrigation ditches.

A voice behind him, scarred by the wind, yelled a question, "Do you think it can be reclaimed?"

Reclaimed? This desert used to be the land that fed a nation. Now, without a steady supply of water, not a single green leaf could be found. The one road was also behind both him and the source of the voice. Two long shadows cast in front of him and over the cracked dirt into the distance.

"Perhaps," he replied, "in the quantum hydration of other farms, your land has been starved. What took you so long to contact us?"

Before the regression of civilization, engineers had learned how to use quantum entanglement to effectively transfer matter. Food could be created from thin air in areas where humans were starving. The soil could be changed to become fertile for growth. However, it had a cost. Incredible amounts of energy were required. In addition, the altered matter was entangled with another matter, called a control, which was required to essentially be sacrificed. If one had enough energy and spare matter, one could seemingly control existence itself.

Overworked land, or even a desert, could be turned into fertile farmland. Water could be purified or even created. In exploration, matter could be recycled between useful forms such as food, air, medicine, electronics, or even a screw driver. This proved especially useful in space exploration, although humanity's progress toward overcoming this final frontier had not reached expectations. Traveling the incredible distances between solar systems or even just our local celestial neighbors just required too large an investment in time. Therefore it was inevitable that the capabilities of quantum entanglement were applied to transportation. Unfortunately, moving life seemed to be far more difficult.

The voice behind came closer, but remained behind him. "Well, this was my father's land, and he had been one of the few to hold out and care for it himself. I hadn't checked on him for a while...but, well, he recently passed away. I hadn't realized what had happened. This used to be a rich and fertile land, producing corn and soybeans. Too bad we can't just quort some crops in here."

"We could, but it would be lifeless." He confirmed. "We can use it to harvest it though."

He thought about how his company had first tested the transportation of tomato plants. The organic material could be moved instantaneously from one favorable location to another. It would appear to arrive in perfect form, with green leaves and red fruit. However, it would soon start to wilt and decompose. During transportation the plant had lost the dynamic essence of life. The matter was the same, but the organized progression of living beings could not so easily be transported. The living things simply became shadows of life.

In highly controversial studies, animals were also sacrificed to the technology. They would always arrive stationary, and no attempts at resuscitation could awaken them. This also limited the ultimate capability of quantum entanglement, the creation of life. Perhaps, someone, somewhere, could have realized that this could be used for the spreading of death. Actually, the entire organism need not be transported to achieve this. It just needed to be scrambled a little.

He knelt down and scooped up a handful of the soil. It felt dry and empty. He let it fall through his fingers back to the ground. Wisps of the earth blew away in the wind as dust.

"...but we can get this land growin' again. Gonna cost you though," he said, still not turning to see the voice. He didn't need to, he had seen the reaction of many land owners and envisioned the grimace of acceptance on the voice's face.

"Ok, let's do it. This is all I have left. Lost my job a few months ago."

"Great, we'll get started when I get back to the office. Let's get back to the airport...I have a flight to catch."

He came out of his thoughts, still leaning against a tree, slowly bending from a steady wind. He and that voice, had no idea of what was coming. How far civilization would fall, and how suddenly. No one knew for sure what had caused it, but he had his own thoughts and suspicions.

However it happened, the capability to harness those technologies of the previous age were all but gone. He recalled that age clearly, and thought that he might be one of the few that still could. It had all happened when he was about half of his current age. He found it strange to think that he had lived as long in the previous Age of Entanglement as he had lived in the current Age of Regression. Yet this period was no longer an Age of Regression to him, it was an Age of Freedom. Most of the other survivors did not use this language and did not know what had caused the *Fall*.

The blue sky now became dark and in a more natural way, not that an eclipse was not natural, but it was rare and unusual. He slowed his pace and began looking for a place to sleep. The sky showed no sign of releasing any rain, and so most any place would do. A soft bed of leaves or even grass would suffice. He checked to make sure no ants or other critters inhabited a possible spot.

He heard some voices in the distance. As he walked, a light sparkled through the forest's vertical population. It emitted from a bonfire in an opening straight ahead. That was the direction he wanted to go, but now a detour was necessary. He veered right and tried to keep a distance that would keep him hidden. In this quiet night, the sound traveled. Perhaps the insects were tired from celebrating the false dusk caused by the eclipse occurring only a few hours before.

He had not yet reached the point tangent to their circle when he could hear the voice more clearly. A younger fellow gave a fiery oration. All he could see was his slender, but strong silhouette. Other humans gathered around the figure, taking the formation of the trees absent in the clearing.

The voice was clear and articulate, "The blinking of the sun gifted a clear omen to us. It is time for us to spread and diffuse across the land. Our work, our preparation, our meditations, have led us to this moment. It is time for humanity to rise again. It is time for one society to form. We have learned from the mistakes of the past..."

Mistakes. So many were made, and they were not so obvious. How could these people, who appeared too young to recall the previous age remember these subtle errors? No history had been recorded that he knew of. The people all seemed to be young enough to be born after the Fall.

"We will teach the chosen how to live and join together. We will form the fibers of a strong fabric that once covered all."

Well, the fabric was far from perfect and it did not cover all. It was discontinuous, with patches of different patterns of weave. The patterns could not be sewn together easily, or with great strength. Some borders were open, while others held tightly with large thick stitches. Even within patches, in areas of homogeneity, the fabric had worn thin and tore. An open edge is where everything could quickly unravel. But what is more beautiful, a tattered patchwork quilt, or a monotone sheet with perfectly crystalline weaves?

"Our fabric will be strong and uniform. Bonding us together in comradery. Others will flock toward us, for the safety, for the knowledge, for the opportunity, for the freedom."

Freedom? This seemed unlikely. Although maybe there was some truth to it. Many philosophers had theorized that the safety and prosperity of society had allowed for art and knowledge to grow. It had laid a fertile soil for new organisms of thought to rise. Yet in some cases the growth consumed the fabric itself. And was there no art before? Paintings and carved rock have been found in the remains of the most primitive societies. Knowledge? Lone hunters were found lying in the ice with exquisite tools, difficult for any human to make. Shadows of humanity still existed in all of its stages of social evolution.

He was now at the shortest distance to the group he would reach while traveling past them. He could see them a little better, but his eyesight was not what it used to be. Men and women, and even some children, were gathered in a circle. All were definitely less than half his age. They all wore similar, but brilliant clothing. Clearly they had made it themselves. Was it the same because they all used the same techniques, or was it fashion? Biologically they were a diverse crowd though. The Fall had dwindled the population so much that for any groups to form meant they had to be very inclusive to all people. There was good in that, even though the words spoken though the trees troubled him.

"Brothers, sisters, let us bring the light to the world before it dims forever as the sun has warned" the voice said in a final statement. Then the social noise grew. He heard conversation and laughing. He had not heard them for some time. It sounded like a foreign language, but it was not.

The light and noise decreased into the patterns of nature. He had not planned to have to walk this late before resting and was very tired. It made him a little less careful in finding a good place to rest. He found a patch of clean, empty grass and no signs of life, so he unrolled his old home onto the ground. He laid part of his pack beneath his head and intertwined his fingers into one of the fraying straps. You never knew what might creep by in the night.

The stars were out and his mind desired to dream. Those people in the woods had twinkled his thoughts. History seemed to have marched backwards, but could it be pushed forward again? We had eaten of the forbidden fruit at the beginning, and another, at the end. Which was good?

Which was evil? They both tasted sweet and could not be expelled once consumed.

<blockquote>
The fruit of Eden

reversed

by the fruit of entanglement,

draws minds

to the roots,

filtering the soil,

feeding eyes

to see the earth

as the garden

again.
</blockquote>

He did not see them, but in the trees were empathetic eyes watching him.

Chapter 3: The Crescents

In the night, he returned in his mind to his island centered in the protection of the coral inside him. To the place he had lost, but subconsciously retained. The sun shone bright there and children played on the beach, building sandcastles that would be razed by the tides. The only safe foundation was far from the ocean and above the line of seaweed marking the high tide. Building there would require carrying wet sand too far. They never learned, or perhaps did not care. Eventually the result was always the same.

Something poked him. The end felt like a broken stick. The poke was not violent though, and just meant to bring him out of his dream. He grunted, but it came out like the growl of a disturbed predator.

"Wake up old man!"

He opened his eyed quickly, and struggled to bring them into focus. It was early, and the sun had not yet risen, but was still in the process of defeating the night. He saw several thin figures.

"Wake up!"

"I *am* awake. Leave me alone." He rasped.

"We need to talk."

He slowly sat up. He saw that the figures each held crescent shaped bows that were nocked and drawn with wood stalk arrows, tipped in stone. His sharpened stick had been kicked away, out of reach. Not really crafted for defense anyway, the stick still sometimes served that purpose. They had also taken his knife.

He examined the figures closely. Four of them surrounded him, two men and two women. They were dressed in the same clean, handmade, clothing he had seen the night before.

"Who are you?" said a striking dark haired, angular woman. She seemed to stare at him as if he were a deer in the woods. He vacantly gazed in return. Maybe he was trying to gather his thoughts.

"He's just an old man," a young man said.

"I think he is old enough to be from the time before. We should bring him back."

Just what he needed, to be drawn into a mess.

"Let me go," he finally said.

"No, we only want to talk. Maybe we can both benefit."

"I need nothing. I have lived this long on my own."

"That individualistic mindset might have been the way previously, but we aim to change things. We are the threads sewing back the tattered remains of humanity. You might like what you see. Get up and follow us."

He sat. They poked him with an arrow.

"Fine. I'll go with you and your merry men."

"What is he talking about?" another whispered. "I have no idea."

As he slowly rose, his joints popped. There was no possibility of escape or chance to fight out of this situation. They still held their crescent bows aimed at him. He slowly packed up his sleeping bag and picked up his pack.

"Follow me," the dark haired woman said.

He stumbled along with them. The three others followed him closely. They did not want anything he had, as they could have taken it by now. He left the sharpened stick behind.

They walked through the woods for a bit until a faint path emerged. The exposed soil hardened and broadened. It clearly was often tread upon. Before long the foreign sounds of social interaction rose on the path in front of them.

From the woodlands emerged a small village. It appeared eerily similar to something he had seen before. This was actually similar to a memory he recalled from the Age of Entanglement. In his mind he was at a museum of human history. Behind rectangular plates of clear glass a village of the original people to inhabit this land had been recreated in impressive detail. Everyone was working on something, except for some younger children. Some were cooking. Some were tanning the hides of animals. Some were weaving baskets. Some were creating pottery. None were idle. He returned to the real world, and the village in front of him was almost identical, but was missing the boundaries of glass. No older people could be seen, at least no one who would remember the previous age.

 Other villages he had seen had continued the conveniences of modern technology, such as electricity, power tools, running water, and the less power consuming appliances. Usually people in groups like this would make use of the still existing, but aging infrastructure. Some complex technologies were difficult to repair and replace (such as computers), but if people had relatively simple skills, others were not. But none of that was here. He wondered why.

 The clothing of the museum's wax figures in his memories was similar in some ways to that of his captors, and consisted mostly of hides woven together. They were relatively modest and not intentionally revealing or sensuous. Some were decorated with beads or dyed. The difference was that some of his captors retained a few items manufactured from the previous age. Some wore shiny pieces of glass that were once used to store information. He recalled that those small pieces of glass could record immense amounts of information. They were said to be nearly indestructible and able to last longer than the lifetime of the planet. All that information was probably still there in the shiny ornamentation. However, one would need the equipment to read it.

Old structures lined the remnants of paved roads. The houses looked much different though. Doors had been removed. Some were decorated differently. Roofing had been repaired with flat stones, or sometimes large leaves.

Several dozen people lived here. More than he had seen together in a while, mostly because he had always managed to avoid them.

As they walked, a few noticed his presence. He saw near the center of the village what appeared to be an old church. Its white paint was almost impossible to see beneath newer coatings of oil and tar like substances, meant to preserve the wood. The cross on the peak of the roof was rusted and bent far to one side.

He was led inside.

Old wooden pews still filled the floor inside, but they had been rearranged in a more circular pattern. In the middle was a fire pit and above it a hole in the roofing, ruggedly crafted.

A fair woman inside was busy repairing some floorboards. She looked up when they entered. "I'll go find Elio," she said and then went running off.

They pointed him to a pew in front and he sat down. It had been a long time since he had sat on a chair with a backing. It was unusual, but restful. He looked around the structure. It appeared to be used now as a meeting place for this group. No books filled the backs of the pews.

Soon the fair woman returned with a man, the same man he had seen speaking to the group in the woods the night before. The man was also young and had a primitive, yet clean cut look.

The dark haired woman who had found him in the woods now presented him. "We found him in the woods not too far away while we were scouting and hunting," she said gripping her spear and peering into the young man's eyes. A strong energy existed between the two. "He had a wood spear and this knife. I thought we should evaluate the situation." The young man nodded and the two stared at each other for a moment too long. With confidence and an unbreakable swagger the young man took a seat opposite to him.

"Hello, thank you for coming here so easily. I am Elio." Elio paused and examined him. This young man seemed to see something familiar within him, as if the past and the future were written on his skin and clothing. For some reason, he could also see his own past in Elio. Something seemed to resonate between them. The way he moved and spoke, reminded him of himself during his age of idyllic naivety so long ago. The way he looked at the dark haired woman reminded him of far-off moments when he had been in love. It was like looking into a mirror of time.

"So you've been traveling alone?"

He nodded.

"You appear to be quite capable of handling yourself. Do you have any destination?"

He said nothing and just stared at a brightly colored stained glass window.

"What is your name?"

He drew a perplexed look. His given name did not matter. Why bother?

"I think I know you. You care only about yourself. You add nothing to humanity. Honestly, you don't smell too good either."

He probably did smell according to the standards he had given up.

"You live, but with no connections, right?" questioned Elio.

Their eyes met briefly.

"I understand. You've seen where we came from. It has to be metamorphic to see how much we've fallen. We want to change that. We want to change life.

You look like a Samson. Alright if I call you that?"

Samson? He had not been called by any name in years. However, resisting would lead to arguing, and arguing would lead to entangling.

Samson knew it was coming, the invitation to contribute and join them. But why would they ask an old man like himself? It seemed that they had already broken apart from the past by leaving others before.

"You could become part of a society again, but I am a little wary of inviting you. We once lived with many who could recall how life was before, but they seemed broken in some way. They had little desire to move forward in a new direction. Maybe they had seen too much darkness. Have you seen too much darkness?"

Samson glanced down to the wood boards.

"Some of those we broke from were also not capable of living this way, without the crutches of technology. Some could not fully adapt. But you...you seem to have adapted.

"So we aim to move in a new direction, but in a direction that will regain the good in what was lost. The rest we must forget. Have you forgotten?"

Of course he had. That ship had hit the teeth of the reef and sunken to the seafloor. Whatever was held in the hull was lost, whether rotten fruit or precious metal. But he had also gained freedom. The moorings and anchors were gone. He was just Samson now.

Elio continued, "I think you have. Maybe the others who found you also saw it."

"You are mistaken." Samson said. "I remember. It is a danger not to. I don't want *any* of it again." Was that a lie? He could not tell anymore.

"So what do we do? Are you a hole in mankind? Will you tear it in a way that cannot be repaired?"

"Just let me go. You will likely never see me again."

"Maybe I was wrong. My gut tells me I am not, but I cannot make you do something you do not want to. Will you do me a favor if I let you go?"

Samson's eyes said that he would not. The tide was going out and the jagged fangs of the reef were slowly emerging.

"Tell others. Tell them that we are here and what we plan."

Samson was not sure where it came from or why he said it, but it came out suddenly: "The sun does not think or foresee, it just is."

He had revealed that he had seen more. Elio was a little surprised and perhaps angered by the statement.

"We all need purpose. We need symbols to strive for. We need direction. You have none. Return to your useless wandering. No one will stop you."

Samson turned and began to rise. The rays of the sun from the window followed the dust swirling around him.

"Here, take these. You could use them here before you leave." The young man took Samson's hand and opened it. He placed within it nine coins. Samson recognized the worn pieces, but each also had been altered. An off center circle had been removed from each coin. The burs and edges had been carefully smoothed and finished. This was not done in one night, but rather with great care. Had the young man known that the eclipse was coming?

Samson turned and left the old church. Outside the scene had not changed much. Several villagers chipped away at stones to make the sharp jagged heads of arrows and spears. Through the door of a machine shop, an old metal press sheared out disks from old coins. The disks were lying on the ground in a pile; their clean, nascent edges reflecting the sun light.

He supposed that he could trade the empty metal Elio had given him for something, like a crescent bow, maybe new clothes, or maybe some food. In other places and interactions he would trade, using things he had plenty of, or no longer needed, for more useful items. For instance, if he had collected several knives, he could trade one for fish hooks or food. Once he had traded a book on agriculture for better boots. But Samson did not this time. For bartering would result in entanglement. That is why Elio gave him the crescent coins. They were his last attempt to ensnare the old man.

Before he left the village, two young children, a girl and a boy, rushed up to Samson. They both had untamed hair, but the boy's was blond and the girl's was dark. He knelt and they placed a crown woven from wildflowers on his brow. He smiled in gratitude, and they ran off.

The sun was still rising, but there was still a chill in the air. Samson turned, placed the sun to his left, and walked toward the dark green forest without hesitation.

He left the round village on one of the many radial paths worn into the tan dirt that dissipated into the shadows. As he did, the children played behind him. He was actually hungry and thirsty, but he wanted to leave as quickly as possible, to avoid being drawn back into the community. He knew that as his distance from the village increased, that the gravity between them would decrease drastically.

Once beyond their view, Samson pulled out his battered canteen and unscrewed the cap. He drank several long swigs. For the moment it seemed to cool a cindering reaction firing inside of him. However, the metal container was almost empty.

He reached into his pack and freed a wild apple. Holding it in his knotted fingers, they seemed to be of the same growth. Both adapting and flowing through the rushing rapids of time. Is that how the untended fruit from the original garden appeared? Only a few apples remained and soon he would need to find more food.

A mountain stream would be a good place to find both. He wondered where the people of the village found their water. He did not recall seeing any wells.

The slope of the land was downward, and that meant he was probably headed in the right direction. Once again, most living things around him did not want to be seen, except for the foliage. The trees reached up to capture the light and divert it before it energized the ground.

Onward he went. Each step grew a little harder because he was tired, thirsty and hungry. The brief interaction with other souls had sent lapping waves on the defensive reef surrounding his being, but some of those waves funneled through gaps and emitted circles of ripples into the lagoon of his soul. Although he did not want it, he had already been entangled to these people. The waves were still small in height, and went mostly unnoticed. However, their frequency did seem to resonate with the protected structures on the island's coast. They were handmade structures on the beach, with teetering towers that would only require a few grains of sand to be removed to cause them to tumble into the salt water.

The land before him solidified from loose soil and pine needles, to solid rock and boulders. Green lichen clung to stone, seemingly unwavering in time. A few ferns also began emerging from the cracks in the stones. The soil in between began to grow a little more moist and coherent. Just a little water allowed the grains of soil to adhere and resist the wind, and the clumsy steps of old boots. This relieved him a little, as he knew water was near.

Soon he heard the repetitive, but random, trickling of water over many stones. He stepped a little faster and soon spotted the brook, pooling in a few terraces on its path downward. The stones exposed to the moving water were slightly worn and polished. The water was as clear as glass, and revealed a few trout. Then he noticed them—precariously placed statues of stacked stones overlooking the pool. They were still, but unstable. The primitive figures appeared to stand guard in silence.

The village must come here for the same reasons as him: water, food…and maybe something else? The statues reflected almost perfect images onto the water, until a tail would strike too close to the surface. He took the wilting woven crown of flowers on his head and placed it on one of the stone figures.

Would the village and its leader, Elio, succeed in removing the eclipse from the world? He did not want to recognize the thought, but it lodged in his mind and grew into a poetic pondering.

Men in the valley
stack pillars
of pebbles,
and grains of sand
into cones,
amid the mountains.

The terrain
seems unaltered,
and always returning
to smooth
from rain and wind;
Until rocks,
alter the flow
of a flood,
to collect the silt
of a new island.

Inspired,
men in the valley,
climb
to place stones
on the apexes,
leaving them taller.

Chapter 4: Dreams

First Samson searched the area around the pooling brook for a long, but undamaged branch. He wanted something slightly green and not weakened by decay. One branch was too large for his fingers to wrap around, so he discarded it. He found a small oak tree and used his knife to cut it free near its base. He quickly shaved the sparse branches free.

"I'm probably doing you a favor buddy," he thought to himself. This oak was striving to survive in the full canopy of many other ancient trees. Its life would have been hard. However, one never knows when a fire or storm might clear the forest allowing such a sapling to reach the light. This severed tree would never be able to see what cards nature had ready to deal.

On the wider end, that was the rooted end of the tree, he began to shave off chips of wood and bark. Soon a sharpened tool revealed itself from the tree.

With a sharp stick, fishing was relatively easily in this transparent water. If Samson stood perfectly still, the fish relaxed dangerously. Then he could jab it quickly with the crafted spear. The fish were not large, so he needed to obtain a good amount of them to be a substantial supply.

Samson used his old knife to quickly gut and clean the fish. He placed them in a plastic bag he had saved. He would cook several soon over a fire and then smoke the rest. However, first he wanted to put some distance between himself, the creek, and the village. He also filled all of his water containers, and cleaned his knife and newly formed stick. The sharp end of the wood was now permanently stained, and would remain that way until he would eventually use it as firewood. It showed some streaking red shadows now in the deep grooves in the grains, but those would slowly turn brown.

He gathered everything and crossed the creek carefully at a location of narrow width, but accelerated flow. Several stones stood withstanding the stream's rush. He carefully and quickly placed his old boots on them as he crossed. On the other side he continued in the same original direction.

He was tired. The walking here was not too tough. The woodland was thick with enormous trees which helped to hide the sun. A tinge of burning color lit the leaves, hinting at the coming of winter, but they were still mostly green.

After walking into the late afternoon he found an open area with some large stones nearby. Some of the stones were too large to move, but could be used as a wind shield and to hold a scaffold for smoking the trout. He cut some green branches from nearby trees to lay across the rocks.

He gathered many small dry twigs and branches that would serve as kindling and tinder to start the fire. He also picked some material that was slightly damp to put on the fire and generate more smoke once it gained a sustainable form.

He layered the fish carefully on the fresh cut structure. They needed to be at just the right height above the fire so that they did not burn or cook, but still received enough heat and smoke to kill any parasites and bacteria. Eating meat infested with that kind of life in the current age could result in a very sick several days or even death.

The current world seemed somewhat like the fish; lots of good people existed to sustain humanity, but still enough parasites thrived to cause serious setbacks. Just a few organisms out of thousands could make the fish seem rancid, just as the society of the current age. However, he hated how most would simply discard it all and label it as lost.

This generalization was similar to the labels used during the previous age of entanglement for distinguishing between generations. Each current generation responsible for keeping the engine churning would label the next generation as being misdirected. Which is interesting, because the older generation raised and taught the incoming one. This phenomena may have also become magnified with the acceleration of communication. Not only had generations been categorized, but entire groups of people with some perceived common trait. There may have been some truth to some generational labels, but the variation among individuals usually overrides the mean.

During the meeting of individuals, these labels are usually proven wrong, but only if one does not bring a rigid preconception. Nonetheless, there are parasites in the meat. The meat is always vulnerable and precautions should always be taken. How much heat and smoke would be required to clean the world? The quantum entanglement was apparently random and did not cleanse it. In addition, with each generation, the bacteria evolve, and may become resistant to antibiotics, smoke and entanglement.

In the current world no systematic way to contain or control the bacteria—or people—existed. In the previous age, there was at least the appearance of control through laws and uniforms. People often lived in this faux belief of security. If they couldn't see or feel the infestation, they could ignore it. Everyone lived differently now, bringing their own fire and sharpening their own defenses.

His mind began to swirl with the smoke passing through the scaffolding and around the trout. He thought of the sun disappearing and those that drew from its mythical energy. He labelled those villagers the crescents. Would they be successful? Could their fire and smoke cleanse the world enough to bring a new age? Were they the next cure, or part of the disease? Even if they were the answer, what would the side effects of the cleansing be? If they succeeded, in one hundred years, how would the practice of following cosmic signs evolve?

In ancient China, the Emperor would be presented amid a fog of smoking incense. This added to his aura and label as an omnipotent ruler. Much of the extravagant ornamentation and rituals fed this same façade. The halls were gilded in gold and adorned with the intricate paintings of mythological events and statues of powerful creatures. The rulers even brought clay armies with them beyond the grave. What was the result? A powerful ruler associated with the strength of the dragon that brought direction and peace to a land. And so many ancient and even modern societies constructed similar hierarchies and structures. Medieval Europe was filled with monarchies ordained by God. Rome's Caesars and Egypt's pharaohs also left proof of their power.

History demonstrated this time and again. But should a flamboyant, articulate, and dictatorial leader who stretches the truth be necessary to bring good to the world? Is a mythical temple high on the mountain necessary, when the actual peak of reality allows one to see truth entirely, unless it is within a cloud?

Part of Samson believed there was still truth in every façade. So much beauty still illuminated the world that he felt something was behind it all. But the pain and changes he had witnessed caused this old idea to become faded in his memories.

The fish were cooking now and the aroma of the cleansed flesh and smoke eased his body. He was very tired. Although he was youthful for his age, he still got tired more quickly than he used to. It had also been a long few days. Interactions with people tested his mind, often stretching him across the sharp growths of the reef within him.

He sat close to the warmth of the fire and against a boulder. The smoke passed around him and his eyes closed to shield themselves. Soon he was asleep and *upon the* deck of an old ship sailing across a vast ocean. The ocean was the world, and the islands places of hope. They were out there somewhere beyond the horizon.

The time was just after the Fall and he had searched all possible places for his family. The Fall happened while he was away, traveling in search of treasure. In his dream this treasure was the lost city of gold. During the Fall the land had sunk under the water, making travel more difficult.

The ship's deck creaked under his boots. The ocean was not still, but followed the steady rhythm of the wind and tides. The leading beam of the ship slowly cut through each wave with a white explosion. He looked down at a map clutched in his hand that for a second appeared to be a collection of memories. What was he searching for? Nothing broke the horizon except the blur of a restless ocean.

He unrolled the old map and he remembered his goal. An island was out there, and marked on the map with a hand written 'X.' The 'X' was not crisp and the paper below it was worn. It appeared to have been erased and rewritten several times. There also seemed to be a few other marks on the map that had been erased from his mind.

He checked his course using a tarnished brass compass. With a slight adjustment of the rudder the bow aligned with the course. The rudder had to actually be left off center to match the wind and fighting current.

Above he heard a flapping of a few of the sails. His alignment of the course had brought the sails out of trim. The tell-tails, small pieces of ribbon on the sails, were flapping. He quickly tied off the wheel with a nearby line of frayed rope.

He traversed the deck and trimmed each sail so that it became tight and collected the wind optimally. Some lines were tightened and some were loosened. As he finished, the ship surged forward with additional urgency.

After a few cold hours in the salty wind, he beheld a peak slowly rising above the horizon. That was his destination, and he felt it somewhere in his gut that this was finally the right one. So many islands had he searched, each one looking surprisingly similar to the previous isolated peaks. He had searched for years. Visiting every port he could recall and find on a chart. Most islands were vacant except for a few survivors. They were survivors of the flood that consumed most of the land and were now isolated by the fierce sea. Unfortunately, they usually weren't much help. Having dealt with so much trauma left some people vacant inside and others merely worried about survival. Some islands were uninhabited, or perhaps deserted. The white beaches kept sweet fruit, indifferent wildlife, and tangles of wilderness, but not what he was searching for.

As the peak, a dead volcano, rose above, the clear water revealed the sharp protection of a blood red reef. He could anchor outside the reef and find another way in, but suddenly he felt an urgency. He continued to adjust the course and trim the sails, the speed brought the vessel slightly more out of the water, decreasing its draft. Perhaps the tide would be high enough to allow his vessel to pass over the living rock of the reef.

As the ship surged forward, its speed appeared to accelerate due to the reef serving as a reference point to judge speed. The last 100 yards came fast. Soon he was peering over the starboard at a bed of intertwining crimson fractal fingers. They began to drag their nails across the hull. The splinters popped as they flaked off one by one. Then the fingers dug in and the vessel came crashing to a halt, but he did not. The mass of his body continued forward, bringing him tumbling into the water. The coral fingers tore open his skin while the waves rolled him over and over again, until finally he regained control.

The reef tagged him with streamers of red as he passed them into the turquoise lagoon. The beach was several hundred yards ahead. Reef sharks suddenly aligned from the magnetic attraction of his blood and headed toward him. He struggled to lift his arms one after the other. The sharks cut through the clear water in easy undulations. He didn't splash much, because he could barely lift his arms out of the water to swim. His motion was more like a wounded turtle seeking rest.

He was almost to shore. It was now shallow enough to stand on the soft sandy bottom. Just before his foot touched the bottom, sharp rows of teeth bit into his side. The shark's motions lost their grace and it thrashed, trying to tear away his flesh. In reflex, he hit the predator in the nose, eyes and gills. It released his body and returned to the same efficient motion that brought it near.

He looked down at a **crescent** *shaped gap crossing from his ribs to his gut. Through the opening he saw his body working and organs pulsating, even though damaged. Then everything went black and all he gazed upon was the corona of the eclipsed sun. The plasma of the corona flowed and pulsated around a perfect circle. The air felt cool and clean. Suddenly, a bright sparkle escaped from one side of* the dark circle and blinded him. The circle was then broken and left incomplete. He squinted.

He awoke lying on his back and staring at a high sun. The air was hot and he felt himself baking on the beach. Turning his head to the side it took time for his pupils to adjust and for his sight to return. The sand around him and especially on one side was a deep red. His wound was still open, and everything hurt.

But then small feet surround him. He lifted his gaze to their faces, but they were blurry and unrecognizable. They looked so familiar...had he found his goal? The three small children smiled at him, but he could only see the curve of their lips and white teeth. Then they began to cover him in sand, starting at his extremities. He did not fight, and really, could not fight. Soon his hands and feet were gone. They worked up his arms and legs to his body. The begin covering his torso, but left his wound and head unobstructed. The sand felt cool on his body, but the sun still cooked his wounds and blinded his eyes. It had a cauterizing effect.

Then a woman of familiar beauty appeared, but again her face lacked its recognizable details. She emerged from the jungle beyond the sand about ten yards away. She peered at him and seemed to nod as if this was an event she had waited for. Amid the blur of her skin, her eyes were vivid and acute. She too smiled but unleashed a stare that went right through his flesh.

Then she said, "Do not worry, we are fine, as you can see. But you are not yet done."

He tried to say something but could barely grunt. He was paralyzed.

She continued, "Your search for us is complete, but something else will begin. You must complete the circle."

Then she knelt next to him. Her hands grasped handfuls of the white sand and sprinkled it on his wound. The salt in the sand stung. Soon the gap was covered, but a blood red crescent dissipated through.

Then she continued and moved her task to his head. First his mouth and nose were covered, and he could not breathe. Next she covered his eyes and as the sand speckled his vision he closed his eyelids. The sun still shown through his lids, but that also ended as the sand grew thicker. Soon all was dark. Samson heard a rustling and a peculiar sound. A sound that was difficult for a man to imitate. It was the sound of raccoons 'talking.'

The high pitched clicks and shrills continued. He slowly opened his eyes just a sliver. The night was still dark and his fire smoked from hot embers. However, several raccoons fed on his fish.

In one fluid motion he drew his knife from his side and lunged it into the nearest creature. It scratched and tried to bite, but not for long. The others scattered into the woods. They had taken a good portion of the fish, but in retribution he had some additional meat. This meant he had to clean the damn thing though.

For a brief moment he recalled the long search he had made. He traveled across unknown lands—that he had only seen before from below wings at 30,000 feet—to the familiar towns of friends and family. For years he had zigzagged across the landscape to find nothing. Then he grew older and entered the new age. The age of entanglement was over. The reef again began to rise from the depths and encase it all.

He was still tired. He quickly, and a bit sloppily gutted the raccoon and threw the entrails far into the woods, which might also keep the hungry occupied and less interested in the fish. He stretched the meat below the fish over the fire, so it would receive a little more heat. He also rebuilt the fire and made it wider, so the food could not easily be reached by the paws of a scavenger. This time he laid down between the fish and the wilderness, while the other side was protected by stone.

The smoke left trails of black carbon on the rocks as it travelled to the stars, just as the stirring thoughts left his mind. Or perhaps they condensed as cosmic matter gathers to form an island planet. The thoughts followed gravity to form words:

Stars
flood the night
until it becomes grey.
Smoke
saturates the flesh
until it is not dead.
Mountains
contain the valley's green life
until it evolves.
Salt and coral
protect the beach
until it regenerates.

Chapter 5: Mountains

Samson had no definite destination, but the climate he sought was at least 400 miles in a general southerly direction and to the ocean. He needed to keep up a steady pace. It would take him over 40 days to travel that far. Without many unforeseen distractions, like the crescent's village, it would not be too difficult. He just needed to get in his routine. Years ago, when he was younger, but still partly entangled, it would take him longer to travel. Of course his youth also enabled more room for errors or mishaps. Now, he had to be careful of every step, although he had also begun to care less.

He was old, especially by the historical averages of human life. He had benefitted from the medical science of the age of entanglement, before it fell. These benefits were actually another form of attachment. One's health and life were often tied to procedures and unnaturally synthesized chemical medicines. The same quantum technology that caused the Fall could also be employed to heal and even regenerate the flesh. They had begun enabling the repair of DNA that had unraveled with age. It had not been perfected, but was definitely effective. Most could not afford the expense of the complete treatments. He was one of those, but at least he could afford something. Others could not afford anything, and simply followed the natural unaltered course of life. Interestingly, these treatments seemed to be promoted and marketed to the people extensively while other healthy practices, such as one's lifestyle and diet, did not gain as much attention. Some people let themselves partake in every dangerous pleasure, knowing and counting on the developing science to save them. When the Fall came, those that remained alive with this mindset did not last long.

Despite these treatments, time and nature were starting to win some battles against his body. Perhaps the decay of time actually accelerated after the treatments ended. The treatments were not permanent, and had to be repeated periodically. They also could not prevent accidents or other events that could cause death or severe wounds. Now his joints began to hurt more, and his eyesight was faltering. His hair had suddenly turned gray a few years ago. His memories had also become harder and harder to recall, but was that nature or a psychological choice?

Even if physically he was years younger than an 'untreated' human of the same age, his mind was not. Time kept accelerating, perhaps due to the lengthening of the datum of experience.

After abandoning his search, he used to wander more randomly, without a defined direction. He was like a molecule, following Brownian motion. He would vibrate and bounce around, following the guidance of food and survival. Most people would repel him. Over time, his average direction of travel would seem to follow some logical pattern. Like molecules diffusing from dense cold to sparse hot, he began following the thermal cycles of the seasons. And now, due to an aging body, in the winter living was easier in the areas farther south.

He also had never wanted to stay put and grow entangling roots into a place. He would stop for a few days in some place, and trade items for goods he lacked. He would also stash some items along the way in case he needed them on future journeys, or if he just tired of carrying them.

In general, Samson would try to avoid mountains when possible. Steep rocks and cliffs always meant more risks of injury during travel. However, plenty of rather large and unavoidable foothills still lie ahead.

On this current journey, few substantial mountains remained on his path. Only a few elevated ridges lie ahead of him on this migration.

On these steep grades the contents of his pack made themselves well known. In his younger, unseasoned days he would carry many useless and yet precious items with him. This included a small collection of books. He had tattered copies of *Useful and Dangerous Plants of North America, Zen and the Art of Motorcycle Maintenance, Heart of Darkness, Lord of the Rings, Robert Frost, The Once and Future King, The Alchemist*, and other random novels he had picked up when rummaging through the ruins and libraries of people gone. He would also burn the printed paper when he was done with it. Some were useful in the beginning because they held knowledge he could use for survival, but that information had embedded in his mind. He soon realized that he did not read them much, and even less and less as he fell deeper into this age.

He also used to write and take notes. Perhaps it helped to keep his sanity. Eventually, the crumpled paper and scribbled words collected in his pack, and began to add weight. He realized that no one would ever read any of those words in this age, so he rid himself of their burden. Some books and writings he used to start his fires. Others he stuffed in depositories staggered along his many paths. Now when these words popped in his head, he would only puzzle them in his mind instead of record them. When they unlocked, the words fled to unknown places.

In the depositories next to these pages, he also stored useful items that he might need on future trips, such as sharpening stones, tools for mending. He also left items which before the Fall were valuable, but now seemed rather worthless, such as jewelry and money.

Other items now weighed down his pack. Most of them he used on nearly a daily basis, such as his cooking pot, knives, sleeping bag, and two lighters that served as fire-starters, along with some lint and waxed wood in case conditions were damp. Other items would be used as needed, such as a hammock, fishing line, tackle, and a sling shot. The fishing line could be used for actual fishing, but it could also be used to bind items together as necessary. If the ground was wet, he would use the hammock to suspend himself above it. The hammock also had a water repelling tarp that would keep him dry in the rain. It sometimes was also simply more comfortable.

He had met other wanderers like himself, and they often asked why he did not carry a firearm. Firearms were heavy and required a good supply of ammunition, while all his slingshot needed was rocks. Slingshots had at one time acquired a reputation to be a child's toy, but they were actually quite deadly. He did keep a few extra rubber bands to replace those that decayed with time. If he kept the bands wet with oil and out of the sun they would last quite long before becoming brittle and snapping. The slingshot was also quiet relative to a firearm which would scare an animal away after one shot. Sometimes the slingshot would allow him to take multiple silent shots at a target.

After the smoked fish and raccoon meat began to run low, he used the slingshot to strike a few squirrels, birds and other small animals. He would mostly just cook them over the fire that he started on most evenings. In the weighing autumn air, the warm meat tasted good and sustained him each day.

He did not cross paths with anyone for weeks and fell back into his routine. His thoughts withdrew behind their normal boundaries, and his dream of crossing the reef left his mind.

The journeys north and south, and life in general, were not always this routine. Even now it was not easy, but he had adapted and had grown comfortable with this nomadic lifestyle, and even enjoyed it at times. Others he had crossed paths with often wondered why he had never settled anywhere. Maybe all those years searching had taken root within him and changed who he was? Some scientists had found that behavior could change the actual genes of a species. This evolution was like the robot changing its own design in order to adapt. He had definitely adapted to the new age, and to all he had lost. The question was, had he evolved or regressed?

Others wondered why he never had companions. He had over the years of this age of freedom only one long term companion. He often wondered if that itself was also a mistake. Her face he could still see, as she still lived in this age. It may have been love, but it probably wasn't. She was definitely a lover, but it never seemed like a sustainable relationship. The companionship was built on convenience and like-mindedness. She had given him pleasure and encouragement, and he did his best to reciprocate. A road took her, providing yet another reason to avoid them. Samson did his best to flush her from his mind, although some of the memories were good ones.

As the large foothills began to flatten and dissipate, he reached one hill in an open area and decided to cross it at its peak. There he found several unobstructed views though the thick trees that allowed him to survey the landscape. Before him were manmade rectangles and grey structures amid the foliage, while behind were the primitive ripples of forest that sculpted him into his current state.

He had a choice, but it rose and was made subconsciously. Did he really want to head to the world of humans again? He had been through many populated and sticky hollers that had almost swallowed him, and brightly illuminated peaks, above shade giving trees, in the thin intoxicating air, that almost made him lose his mind. His body slowly degraded with each year's journey.

The sun was beginning to set and the colors broke apart from the homogeneous white light into beautiful layers of orange, red, pink and blue. A few clouds crossed these colors and were painted by them. One did not just view these moments, you were a part of them, and were perhaps entangled within them. Sometimes he would forget to partake in these moments, but he definitely did so more than those living enclosed—by walls, trees and mountains.

As the sun fell below the horizon, a few of the square structures illuminated. They looked like lighthouses on a sea of dark green rolling waves. A lighthouse warns vessels of shallow water and rocks. Or were they beacons, marking distant harbors? Maybe they played both roles.

He was tired and found a decent clearing perfect for making camp. He gathered some dry wood of different sizes and layered them from small to large so that they would catch fire. He drew out the lighter he had been using and spun the flint wheel with his thumb. It sparked, but no flame synthesized. He brought the clear plastic body of the lighter up in front of the brightening moon. No fluid was left. He dug through his pack for another lighter and used it to start the fire. He did not like being down to his backup lighter and would have to find more fluid or a new lighter. There was sure to be some amid the remnants of the tangled world that lay ahead on his path.

On the growing fire he boiled some water and made some tea. He was very tired, and soon fell asleep.

He awoke in what seemed an instant later to the light impacts of water droplets. The fire steamed and exhaled with each burst of fluid. He wasn't sure how long until daylight arrived, but he was no longer tired. Soon his gear was packed and ready to carry. He also drew out a water jug and a plastic cone he had fashioned long ago from a parka and strands of thin wire. The droplets grew in number and frequency. He unfolded the cone and fit it onto the mouth of the water jug. He placed it with the cone open to the sky in an outer pocket of his pack. He then stood up, grabbed his current walking stick, and continued his journey. The water felt refreshing and cleansing. The air was not cold and he even removed his jacket a few times to expose himself to the rain.

The rain continued for days with a light, but relentless, drizzle that wet the world. The terrain flattened and became muddy. His boots left deep prints in the muck. At night he would wrap himself in the hammock to stay dry.

He soon reached a familiar large flat granite rock formation. One of the stashes he had left and built up over the years was nearby. The flat rock was forever scarred by many generations, and especially from the age of entanglement. Some had painted their message, and most of those had faded or worn away considerably, but a few had actually carved into the stone. Some proclaimed messages of love, while others took natural rock formations and added features to create images. From an oval shaped mark hung legs that either rendered it to look like the symbol pi or a jellyfish. One set of faint speckles of paint appeared to form the word "Welcome." Man had even succeeded in entangling nature forever. However, this had probably occurred over the entire history of man, and not just in certain ages. Ancient man had left marks on stone that had endured thousands of years. These ancient messages actually succeeded in revealing their existence to modern man. These more recent marks reminded him of the previous modern age.

He followed the flat rock and walked by stagnant puddles of algae surrounded by growths of lichen. Some bloomed in vibrant colers of red that seemed to exist as a warning. The water in these pools was definitely not fit to consume. The sun warmed the water and helped to generate the growth of these pockets of life.

A few bits of brave foliage had even succeeded in rooting within pockets of loose soil on the rock. Despite all odds, they had thrived on a terrain, alien to the surrounding forests of green. It made him feel as if he was temporarily leaving the earthly world.

Samson followed the flat rock to a ledge on the outer boundary of the formation. He could tell by a faintly carved mark, that this was definitely the spot. He reached his arm over the edge and into a crevice under the ledge. He pulled out a sealed plastic container. The container had grown mold on the outside. Its dimensions were about 1ft by 2ft and half a foot deep. He unfastened the latches on the edges easily. He seemed to recall that in past years these latches did not open so easily due to the debris and growth around them.

The contents of the container were clean and dry. He tilted the lid to shield the contents from the misty rain. Inside was a sealed bottle of whiskey, a bottle of honey, a jar of dried beans, a new knife, loose sheets of scribbled upon paper, a copy of *Brave New World*, a few other texts, and something new...a glossy brochure with worn edges protruding from the pages of the book. Some of these were items he had left on previous springtime journeys toward the mountains.

"Figures, no lighters," he thought to himself, disregarding the brochure. Someone must have found his stash and left it. He took out the book and opened it to the page marked by the brochure. The pages parted near the end of the novel, and John the Savage had just decided to escape from the utopian society. He read a few lines, "The Savage had chosen as his hermitage the old lighthouse which stood on the crest of the hill between Puttenham and Elstead." He perused the words he had read before and came upon "When the morning came, he felt he had earned the right to inhabit the lighthouse; yet, even though there still was glass in most of the windows, even though the view from the platform was so fine. For the very reason why he had chosen the lighthouse had become almost instantly a reason for going somewhere else." A few more pages slipped past his fingers..."He had sworn to remember, he had sworn unceasingly to make amends. And there was he, sitting happily over his bow-stave, singing, actually singing...."

He felt the invisible grab of something coarse and salty on his red innards, and abruptly shut the book. He pulled free the brochure, crumpled up a few loose sheets of tarnished paper, grabbed the bottle of whiskey and stuffed them in his pockets. The plastic container closed with a deep thump and he returned it to its normal resting place.

He left the geological monument and soon settled in for the night. The rain was still falling in a relentlessly steady rate that had penetrated and saturated the air itself. He used the loose paper to start a hungry fire, and dry the damp wood he placed on it, before consuming it. He took several swigs from the whiskey bottle. He had decided that he was no longer saving it for anything, and if he had been, the likelihood of that event occurring had become minuscule. It could have also been used to help sterilize any wounds that were likely to occur from time to time. If it happened now, he might actually welcome a beginning to the end. As the clear liquid passed his lips, the soothing burn in his throat was one he had not felt in sometime.

He also took out the brochure and held it close to the fire. It showed a picturesque landscape of cottages facing green water, and a lighthouse in the distance. The lighthouse had large horizontal stripes of red and white. The text printed on the glossy but tattered paper read "Visit Harbourtown." Below the large joyous text and within the folded pages details about the resort, activities, restaurants, and directions were given, along with a small map. Clearly, this was all from a previous age. Handwritten on the cover was also the note:

> Join us and contribute to the lighting of the new world.

Samson pondered the note for a few moments and then tossed it in the fire. The paper curled and the glossy images seemed to first brown and then burn from the inside. When it fully caught fire, the light of the flames suddenly brightened and then died in a thick plume of smoke.

The alcohol had now taken its effect. It brought a sweet calm. The substance had always made cryptic thoughts flow and seem more reasonable.

> The lighthouse,
> a controlled flame
> suspended in the night,
> marks the rocks
> or is it a beacon
> guiding us to the harbor?
> Or is it both?

Chapter 6: The Mean Free Path of Man

Molecules floating in a gas will only interact on occasion, and these interactions often drastically change their course. This is what induces the random dance of Brownian motion that the erratic molecules follow. The average distance a molecule would travel between these interactions is called the mean free path. The distance grows and shrinks with temperature and pressure.

In this age, wanderers like himself might not see someone for great amounts time and distance. However, unlike the molecule, man has some control over this distance. When in a condensed populated area, impact was more likely. At higher speeds of travel, the distance covered is farther and the crossing over the paths of others is more frequent.

He estimated over the years that only about one in every thousand people survived the quantum entanglement disease. Many others also perished due to indirect effects, such as being in a vehicle without a driver. Therefore the mean free path of man (how long a man would travel or live before meeting another man) had increased immensely after the Fall. Nonetheless, on occasion interactions could not be avoided.

The steady rain had stopped for at least a little while, and the sun emerged from behind the clouds. Samson had walked at a leisurely pace for a couple of days and come across a town that seemed more deserted than usual. At night, the town emitted no light and no sounds into the woods. He thought that this might be a good opportunity to resupply and find a few more lighters. At the edge of the town a stark remnant of the previous age emerged before him. What rose was an enormous *super* store that carried essentially everything people used to need and want. It had probably evolved from the general stores that used to be located within every small downtown. The large structure was not constructed particularly well, and the elements had taken a toll on it. The thin metal walls and roof of the rectangular structure had rusted through in some areas. The enormous sign that had once illuminated in vivid colors of blue and red was now dark and the colors faded to gray.

Surrounding the store was a flat asphalt parking lot. A few vehicles remained parked. They all had flat tires and faded paint and dirt on any surviving glass and in crevices. He was not worried about running into the passengers. The lines painted on the lot were all but gone and in places cracks had opened and allowed foliage to erupt from them.

Grasses and even some small trees rose scattered across the flat.

Next to the store was a school and a playground. The fence around the playground was rusted and barely holding off the force of gravity. Only the metal chains dangled from the swing set frames, and creaked in the wind. Other decaying small houses also surrounded the area. Some of them were almost completely hidden behind bushes and the shade of large oaks.

He left the cover of the forest and began across the parking lot. This was the most dangerous part. Any type of concrete or asphalt sculpted ground was often the hunting grounds for the predators of this age. He felt like a gazelle...no, more like a slow elephant making his way to a watering hole. He kept a sharp eye for hidden vehicles or others in hiding. The heat from the asphalt rose up against him, but the wind also whipped across it without any obstructions to stand in its way.

He made it across without incidence and relaxed a little. The doors of the store were actually intact, which was a good sign. The door creaked when he opened it. The grocery department of the store of course had been looted long ago. He remembered when disasters and false threats would cause people to frenzy on these stores like sharks on an injured whale. The food section of the store would be empty of items like bread and milk almost immediately. This he found humorous, because many other items in the store would ultimately prove to be more useful in a true crisis.

The inside of the store was dark and light only dissipated across it from the few windows and doors at the front. At night it would be very difficult to see. The remains of several human shoppers also met him in the aisles, but they were from long ago and all that remained were bones, and brown stains on the floor from the decayed flesh. In more populated places these skeletons would have been removed or put to rest somewhere. And if indeed only one out of a thousand survived, a town or city would have to be very large to retain a significant population after the Fall.

He first stopped by the kitchen section and found a new knife that could replace his, whose blade was slowly wearing thin with each sharpening. Next he headed to the 'outdoor cookout' section of the store. Several small sized solar and kinetically powered flashlight and radio devices still hung on wired displays. They also had a microphone so that a voice log could be recorded in a survival situation. He had no need for the voice recording, but it was small and the light would be useful, so he grabbed one. A few larger lighters still remained in their yellowing packaging. He quickly threw them in his pack, but one missed and fell to the ground. The sound echoed through the store. Almost simultaneously he heard what sounded like a few fast footsteps on the concrete floor. Whatever was out there in the shadows was definitely larger than a rodent.

Just what he needed. He wanted to get out of there without any contact and so quickly made his way to the side door of the once Lawn and Garden department. He passed by some garden tools and grabbed a hoe on a five foot handle and discarded the stick he had been carrying.

He made it to the door, but thought he heard scurrying behind him. It sounded almost more like an animal than an adult human. He made it to the door. Unfortunately this one was chained shut. Fortunately the door held large panes of glass. Looking back he spotted something crouching in the shadows. He was not scared, but did not want to deal with anything unnecessarily.

He raised the hoe to his side and brought it against the glass like a baseball bat. It made a loud crack. The glass broke, but did not shatter free of the door frame. He looked back and the figure was gone. Perhaps the noise had scared it away. He bashed the glass a few more times and broke it loose. He continued until none was left and his stout body fit the opening with ease. He kept the hoe and exited.

Samson paced a few steps into the lot and looked back. A shadow of a small figure came closer and then crouched through the broken glass. A girl of maybe eleven or twelve years of age emerged, but Samson was a poor judge of age. She was skinny, but still healthy. Her skin was pale, and she had hair as dark as the night. Her clothing was a little worn and dirty, but had been mended at some time. She wore blue jeans that had the scars of tears around the knees. Threads were unravelling around her shoes. She wore a handmade long sleeve, rugged shirt that looked almost like a sweater due to the large threads used to make it. She couldn't have been there alone, so he turned and began to walk away at a brisk pace.

The clouds had returned and the rain began to fall again. Steam rose from the asphalt. He left the lot and headed onto a street lined with aging houses. He glanced back. The girl was following at a safe distance.

He did not see any signs of inhabitants and so continued down the road. The houses were tempting sanctuaries to stay in until the rain passed. He looked to the sky and could see a clear line of dark clouds slowly rolling in. This probably meant a cold front and the temperatures would be dropping soon.

He was about six houses down and he heard a rock impact the road near his feet. The girl had thrown it at him! He looked back and she was pointing toward the third house and waving her arm to him in a welcoming gesture. He paused.

There was something inverted or transposed about her. He decided to follow her to at least get out of the rain tonight. He walked back to her. She was trembling and clearly afraid, but was still clearly in control of her actions. Why would she invite him in if she was afraid?

The house was covered by red brick, and the roof and windows also appeared to be intact. With just one floor, the home was not large. The painted surfaces were peeling in some areas, but some spots had been covered by what appeared to be a wax or tar.

She followed a path to the front door through an overgrown lawn that now sustained tall grasses and a thicket of bushes. She did not contact a single leaf and walked to the house with a grace reserved for wild animals in nature. Even at her age she was confident and an extension of the natural workings of the world. She turned a tarnished knob and opened the door.

To him, the untamed lawn was another sign of freedom. In the age of entanglement each lawn in front of each house had evolved to a common blueprint of genetically modified grass and ornamental bushes. The lush, soft grass could grow under almost any amount of sunlight and in a wide range of climates, but it still required trimming to obtain the flat artificial appearance of proper folks of the previous age. How many trips he had once made to a lawn and garden department identical to the one he had just escaped from. Now the land was free and regressing to its own state. The leaves were still green, but would soon turn brown with the arrival of winter. She opened the door and waved for him to enter. He also followed the path, and caused many leaves to rustle as they contacted his worn figure. Then he trudged into the house.

The inside of the house was in good condition, considering its age. He had not been in a house like this in many years, and he had to admit that it was a pleasant feeling. From the front door foyer, on the left was the dining room and on the right was a slightly larger living room. The dining room was painted red, but a few cracks and peeled spots revealed the pale drywall underneath. A wooden table and chairs still showed a glowing finish. A family picture hung on the wall of a mother, father and two children, but neither were the girl or even had a resemblance to her.

The girl had left and was doing something farther in the house, which was dark without any electrical lighting. He turned to the right, leaned his pack and hoe against the wall, and sat down on a blue sagging couch in the living room. The hoe was within reach. Behind him was a window to the untamed front yard. The light entering the house was filtered by the leaves, and the day was already cloudy, so the lighting was poor. A small table in stood front of him and a flat black screen hung on the wall. The only function the screen served now was that of a flawed mirror.

He opened a drawer of the table to find a small collection of glossy printed magazines. These printed magazines were losing popularity even before the Fall, and were an unusual find. One was a science magazine celebrating one of the earliest quantum entanglement successes. Scientists in China had entangled matter on earth with that on a satellite in orbit. On the cover it showed a still from the early television show Star Trek. The characters of the show were partly transparent and filled with sparkling bits of light.

Another magazine was about the popular culture of motion pictures and music. On the cover posed a female singer holding a microphone in a jeweled dress that was sparkling from the stage lights. The caption read, "Ascending to the Top!"

The girl returned with a lit candle and a mug of a hot beverage that she set on the table in front of Samson.

"Thank you," he said.

She left and returned with her own mug and sat down in a chair in a corner opposite from the couch. Her presence pulled on the reef and water of his soul. Her gravity was perpendicular to his consciousness and caused his mental waters to recede and expose the sharp protective peaks of the red coral.

"Why did you ask me to join you?" he asked.

She shrugged her shoulders.

He did not hear any other noises or voices in the house. It seemed that her parents were not here.

"Where are your parents?"

The question did not receive any response and she merely looked down at the mug in her hands. After a moment, she took a deep gulp. He also drank his beverage. It had a slightly bitter taste, but had been sweetened by some kind of citrus fruit.

She did not carry any weapon, at least ones that were unconcealed, but did seem aware of the possible danger of the situation. Her behavior appeared to compliment his own demeanor.

She did not watch, and maybe never even heard of the planes falling from the sky, of the factories and power plants failing and self-destructing, without engineers there to control and repair them. Of hospitals going dark and patients waiting for doctors and nurses who would never return. Of farmland, whose crops succumbed to parasites and the weather, and slowly returned to forest. Of the bodies of so many decaying where they died. Of the manufactured goods and fuel slowly being depleted or decaying on the shelf. Of people left without the skills or will to survive on their own.

She was untainted by the brutal history of the world, and was still a sapling in the forest, growing up toward the remaining light. Others, already grown and rigid, could not so easily adapt. She was pure and undefined. She was truly untainted and untamed in a time of freedom.

She had already grown into and adapted to fit and utilize the contorted light still piercing the forest canopy. She could follow the synergistic trails of the world, while the older generations still worked to bludgeon paths into the world that they could follow. And she continued to grow into it, rooting into it and strengthening.

The intermediate generation between her and Samson bridged the two. The village of the Crescents, made mostly of this generation, recognized this and tried to control the process of adaptation by cutting themselves away and starting over. It remained to be seen if they would succeed.

How had he adapted and survived? He seemed to be the exception to the divides between the generations.

The time leading to the age of entanglement some labeled as the age of entitlement. Humanity had grown dependent on the machinery of the man-made world to survive and be content. But now, it was clear that nature gave no entitlement to anyone. It did not care about or recognize these generations, or maybe they did not exist at all, except in the human mind.

The sun was falling lower and in the dark the girl's face glowed like the moon. The room was also silent like the night sky. The rain never arrived. They finished their tea without disrupting the silence.

She left and came back with two bowls of hot stew. It tasted like squirrel, along with some carrots and squash. He had to admit that it tasted good. Soon the bowls were empty and she collected them. She motioned to him to follow.

He followed her through the unlit hallway into a kitchen that had a large window overlooking a backyard. The backyard was surrounded by other backyards filled with grass and a mixture of indigenous and exotic foliage. Several young oak trees had begun their quest to cover the freed landscape, and the planted ornamental bushes struggled to survive.

The yard behind this house was cleared and uncovered though. It had been filled with a garden of a variety of vegetables. Since this was the end of the growing season, much of the plot had already been harvested, and only the cracked holes of pulled plants remained.

The kitchen held an area that had been altered into a hearth with a flume bringing the smoke outside the house. The kitchen still had an old sink, but the faucet had been removed because there was no pressurized water. The water still did flow down the drain and exit into a sewer pipe. A few large plastic containers of water lie on the worn blue tile floor that she had brought from some unknown source.

In a pantry next to the kitchen was a stock pile of food for the winter. Plenty of preserved meats and jarred vegetables lined the shelves. Some fresh items were also lying in baskets on the shelf. The bounty included dried and cured meats, dried beans, grains, potatoes, apples, carrots, squashes, and a variety of other items.

This impressed Samson. "You did this all yourself?"

She just nodded.

A backpack leaned against the wall that also seemed to be partially prepared for a long journey. He wondered what she was planning. The food and the pack seemed to be in contradiction. He was positive that her parents were not here, but he was not sure for how long.

He then realized the entanglement occurring in this intersection. Her gravity was pulling him off path, even though he did not have a defined course. He was no longer under the simple control of natural forces. Did she expect anything from him?

"Planning on a trip?" He asked.

She just shrugged her shoulders and went to the pantry, gathered a collection of items and put them into a basket and gave them to him.

Holding the basket he said, "You don't want to go with me. I travel alone and won't go where you want to. My destination is not yours."

She did not seem to be affected by his statement and walked away unscathed with the bowls and cups to wash. He went to the back door and headed out into the garden. The sky was now dark. The moon and a few oil lamps inside the house now provided the only light. He looked up at the sky. The clouds had opened to reveal the pale disk and some stars in the darker parts of the sky. Those stars would not have been visible and drowned out by artificial light during the previous age before the Fall. Words condensed in his mind from the sparkling dust above.

The scars

of our impacts

against others' orbits

glow

and slowly heal

and sift flat

under the steady vibrations

of collisions

to a wrinkled face

in the night sky.

Chapter 7: Reflections

Samson woke early. He had slept on the couch in the same room that they had eaten the night before. The room was relatively dark because the sun was rising onto the opposite side of the house.

He worried about becoming entangled with the life of this girl. He appreciated the hospitality, but it was time to leave. She seemed to have done quite well on her own regardless.

He filled his pack with the food she had given to him the night before. Ready to go, he thought that perhaps he should leave something as a show of appreciation, without risking the creation of a connection.

His calloused and dirty hands searched through his pockets. There they were, the crescent cut coins given to him earlier in his journey. He pulled them out. To him they were worthless, but maybe she would see some value in them. They slid from his hand onto the image of the singer and the sparkling dress. A few rolled off the magazine and spiraled around until they then clanged flat on the table and fell silent.

Pack on and hoe in hand, he opened the door slowly and headed out into the narrow path that led back to the world. His arms and legs brushed against the leaves and left them fluttering behind him.

Before exiting the path completely, he crouched behind a full hydrangea. Its voluptuous bulbs of flowers indicated that it was not a hydrangea native to North America. He peered out to the road. A thick fog floated along the flat landscape, but a person would rise above its shallow depth like the peak of a mountain. He saw no one.

He rose and immersed himself in the fog. A vacant trail followed him as he walked along the road in the direction away from the super store. The world was silent except for the chirping of a few birds and the rustling of squirrels, but it sounded different than in the deep forest. The natural world here was still partly dominated by the man-made alterations.

The houses ended where the small road met a larger one. He looked for a way to escape the roads and pavement as soon as possible. Across the road lie the worn gray stones of a large city cemetery. Past the cemetery were the tops of large trees and what appeared to be the edge of a wooded area. He looked down and took his first step in that direction.

Then he heard a door close behind him.

"Dammit," he murmured to himself.

He looked back and the girl was heading his way through the thick fog, wearing the pack he had seen the night before. The fog gathered ahead of her like soil ahead of a plow, or water ahead of the bow of a boat.

He might as well wait. He could tell that this one would follow him if she wanted to, no matter what he did.

She stopped several houses down at one that he had not noticed before because of the fog. In front of her stood the hollowed out frame of a house that had burned down. It did not appear to have happened that long ago. Smoke still seemed to drift from the ashes, or it could have just been the fog. She looked at the house for a few moments and then fell to her knees. She placed on the ground what appeared to be a terracotta pot holding a deep green plant. She was not sobbing, but rather saying goodbye. She clutched some soil from the yard and let it fall from her hands through the fog and back to the earth.

This must have been her family's house and she must have lost them in the fire. They probably were also both survivors of the Fall and most likely had met after it had occurred. They had raised the next generation of mankind, and based on what he had seen, they had done a good job. Or perhaps this generation was already naturally adept to the world out of necessity.

Samson decided to move on. If she wanted to follow, she would, but he was not going to make it unnecessarily easy. He was not sure if he wanted any sort of companion anyway.

He turned and walked toward the woods through the many tombstones, half consumed by the fog and the other half worn by time and overgrown by grasses and vines. The coarse arches of the stones were all that showed above the mist in some places.

Soon, the girl and the houses behind him disappeared from sight. He thought about what she would do as his figure disappeared into the fog.

He reached the edge of the cemetery and the beginning of the woods. A path cut into the woods not far from him. The mist drifted into a forest of old hickory trees, water oaks and sweetgums. The water oaks were large and stoic, acting as a strong elderly figure. The sweetgums left their starry ball of seeds over the ground, alongside the hard shells of the hickories. These trees usually indicated a marsh or water lay nearby.

The path led to an opening in the woods. A very large rectangular pit had been dug in the opening. Water had collected and stagnated in the pit for many years. Brown and green algae and aquatic plants grew and thickened the water. White rounded shapes protruded from the green water. They must be rocks. But then Samson looked closer. They were not rocks, they were human bones. The curved surfaces of sockets and articular joints peaked above the water. Amid the mud, what appeared to be the corner of a skull and eye socket peered up at him.

The remains left him in a solemn trance for several minutes. Soon the silence broke with the sound of footsteps heading up the same path. The girl emerged. She stopped next to him and looked into the pit and up at him. Did she know what this was? These were the remains of a time before she was born. She probably had wandered in the woods and had found this on her own before. The question was if anyone had explained it to her. It was not his job to inquire or to do so though.

She looked up at him and her slouching body language seemed to confirm his thoughts. Her look seemed to state that she had seen it and knew about what had happened to these people.

They stayed a few more moments and then the girl looked past the pit and identified where the path continued to the south. She left and went down the path without saying a word.

Samson remained, gazing down at the pit. The decaying bones seemed to speak to him more clearly now, but he did not want to believe them. However, they spoke as ghosts do, to the soul of the man. He did not realize it, but they had planted something there in him, or perhaps just released something that he built up over the years. Like a dam with a small hole, the leak was sprung.

He turned toward the path and left.

It did not take too long for him to catch up to the girl, although once he did, she quickened her pace. He looked up toward the sun that had broken through the fog and clouds. She was heading south. At least they were in agreement about something, even if it was in silence.

The two walked over smaller hills and across creeks. They had plenty of food, in fact almost more than they could carry, so there was no reason to stop when wildlife was spotted.

That night they made camp in a clearing amid some tall longleaf pines. Their tall trunks were spread far apart from each other across the grassy area. At a height well above the humans, their thin leaves exploded like fireworks in front of the moon.

Samson used the new lighter to start a fire from some fallen branches of the pine. The wood was light and burned quickly and brightly. It did not last long before its fibers reduced to ashes, so they had to cook quickly. The girl cooked some of the more perishable meat and vegetables first.

Soon they were crouched over their food and eating. Samson caught her looking across at him through the thick smoke of the pine fueled fire.

"You are even quieter than I am," he said. "At least with words you are."

She just continued to eat.

"Well, if you're going to take the same path, we need to communicate."

She was still eating, but had to be listening.

"You seemed to be able to handle yourself out here, but I suggest that I take the lead when making decisions."

She still ate.

He finally asked, "What is your name?"

She shook her head as if to say she was not yet ready to reveal that.

"Fair enough, I don't enjoy telling everyone who I am either. However, we might need to call or yell to each other if trouble arises. Some fool a while back gave me the name Samson, I guess you can call me that." The moon above them continued its primal pull on his blood.

"How 'bout I call you Selene?"

She finally responded to him and shrugged as if it didn't matter.

"I guess that's it," he said.

They continued south for several days. Their food supply remained plentiful, but they started to hunt along the path. Selene revealed her weapon of choice, an atlatl—a deadly device used to throw a small spear using a lever like stick carved with a pocket on the end to hold the base of the spear. The lever mechanically amplified the speed that transferred from the arm and wrist of the user. Samson had seen them before and knew that great skill and practice were required to use one well, but once mastered, it was unequaled compared to other primitive weapons. He recalled hearing that the first people of this land had created and used the atlatl.

Selene was successful in killing several small animals that added some protein to their meals. She was actually proving her worth.

On the third day of their journey they reached a large lake. Samson seemed to have remembered reaching this lake sometime before, but he may have just changed his route on most occasions. They walked down to the water and filled their containers with water that they would boil later.

Samson looked across the lake. The lake was about a mile across and made by man long ago. The dam retaining the water must still be intact. The air was dead and the trees across the lake and close to him reflected perfectly on the water. Some of their leaves had already been painted in yellow, orange and red by the cool air. Their predecessors, including ancestors, siblings, and even offspring, had fallen into the water in some places due to erosion of the shore. Others had not fallen in, but had been submerged a long time ago when the river was dammed to create the lake. The bare knuckles of their branches grasped for the air from their waterlogged trunks. They were the ghosts of those who had crossed into another realm calling back through a transparent boundary.

Then the wind began to blow and ripples caused the jagged lines of the trees' images to curve and bend. He looked down at his image in the water as it began to bend and contort. The soft wood spirits below the surface also disappeared under the ripples.

A few houses and broken down shelters remained scattered along the edges of the lake. Protruding from the houses were long wooden docks that stretched out over the glassy lake. They were like fat hairs dangling into the water.

Samson turned to the left and to the right, peering out into the long extension of the lake. Selene also noticed the long distance.

"I've walked around this lake before. It is a long hike. I've never gone across," He remarked.

Selene began walking along the shore toward the East. It looked like farther down that the shore shifted toward a southeastern direction.

Samson picked up a thin flat rock from the ground and threw it with a tight spin across the water. The pebble skipped seven times before succumbing to its lack of buoyancy. It sank deeper into the abyss in a rocking motion. The rock drifted out of sight and was now merely a lost concept in his mind. As the ripples reached the shore, he turned to follow Selene along the shore.

They walked past several worn down and collapsed houses. Most of the docks were empty. Some had boats that were half sunk. Samson thought they could take one of these and paddle or even sail across the lake. He thought to stop Selene to convey this thought, but she was already three docks ahead of him. Then a boat floating ahead of him came into view. Selene had nearly reached the aluminum pontoon boat, partially tinted in the green of aquatic growth. A flat platform was lifted above the water by two long aluminum pontoons that were cylindrical in shape except on their front where they took on a V-shape to cut through the water.

The homestead next to the dock appeared to be in active use. The old home was standing and had been repaired on the roof in several places by wood shingles over a tin roof. Hanging on a few trees were some skins and cured meat. A small garden also had been cultivated, but now had been mostly harvested and contained only cracked and empty soil.

He then noticed a sign on the shore next to him that said "Ferry" and had an arrow pointing toward the dock with the floating boat. He reached the homestead of the ferry and spotted another old sign above the dock that had been coarsely carved into it the words,

"Karon's Ferry Service"

The wood of the dock was bleached by the sun and covered by loose splinters. A spotted yellow brass bell hung below the sign with a tattered rope falling limp below it.

Selene looked at Samson and then at the bell. "Hold on," he said, also raising his hand. He slid the garden hoe into a strap on his pack. Next, he took out his slingshot from has pack and found a hard rock from the ground. Selene followed suit and prepared the atlatl in her hands by balancing a small spear on the bottom of her right forearm as she raised the lever arm back behind her. With her left arm she rang the bell.

They heard a dog barking from the house and then a voice yelling, "I'm coming, hold your horses."

A tall and lanky old man emerged from the house out of a creaky door. He wore a faded black jacket with a tattered hood on his head. A black dog, a retriever mix, walked close by his side, but still was barking with excitement.

"Whoa, whoa. Never mind ole' Sticks. He just likes to welcome visitors, or should I say clients? He's Sticks 'cause he never leaves my side."

"You Karen?" Samson blurted.

"You mean Karon? Yeah, my parents' idea of a way to harden me I figure. Kinda like that Johnny Cash song," he said pausing on a memory. "Haven't heard that song in a long while."

The sun crept closer to the horizon across the lake and the air began to cool. The colors of the sky were beginning their brilliant finale to the day.

"Y'all want to cross now, 'er wait till tomorrer? Today will cost you extra."

Selene lowered the atlatl, and removed some fresh meat and vegetables from her pack. She raised them toward the man.

"Do it look like I need food?" he said, while pointing a bony finger toward his garden.

Selene reached down in an outer pocket of her pack and pulled out one of the largest crescent cut coins. She must have collected them from the table before they had left the house.

"What we have here?" the man said holding out his pale hand. She placed the coin in his palm. He peered down it and then rolled it in his knotted fingers. His fingers slowly closed over the coin and into a possessive fist.

"I've seen one of these 'fore! It'll do, along with the food. Come along. Let's get goin' so I can get back before dark."

The man in the black clothing walked with almost a limp toward the flat pontoon boat. He picked up a large pole with a wide paddle on one end.

"Y'all comin'?" he said gesturing from the boat. Samson and Selene went out on the dock and stepped onto the boat. When Selene stepped onto it, the craft barely rocked, but when Samson pressed his weight down it tilted and then fluctuated several times before adjusting to the new load.

The old man in black carefully untied several frayed and mildewed ropes from heavily corroded and pitted metal cleats. He threw the moorings to the dock and pushed off with the pole. At first he used the pole to press against the muddy lake bottom, pushing the boat along. His motion changed to a smooth paddling of the water once the lake bottom became too deep. The elements were still except for the churning of the water. The sun cut deep wounds in the sky and it became red.

Selene came up to Samson and forcefully placed the remaining eight crescent coins in Samson's hand. He did not want them, but she did not give him a chance to resist. He simply nodded back to her.

Samson watched the old dock they departed from drift away and the shore of reflections across the lake enlarge and fill in with more detail. Selene was looking ahead with a slight breeze against her hair. He looked down at the dark water and thought of the submerged trees 100 feet below, where dry land had once been. He thought of the skulls and bones in the mud, and his soul awoke a little. He could not stop the thoughts in his mind.

The boundary is flat
on the river.

Roots erode;
and trees cross the realm,
extending
the bare knuckles
of their bony fingers
to the travelers
above.

The swirling knots
of the waterlogged wood
stare across
and speak
to the ringed cores
of the survivors.

The fibrous matter
separates
from the soul
in the dark depths.

We wallow in the mud,
with unburied bones,
exposed,
and leaving no need
for chiseled tombstones.

Chapter 8: Sticks

The old man in black used his long arms to move the platform across the lake. The sky had turned nearly black now and a mist was creeping in across the land and water. He moored at a dock just as decrepit as the one they had left from. He did not tie to the dock, but just simply raised his long fingers and pointed his passengers ashore. His dog, Sticks, actually followed Selene and Samson onto the dock.

"Sticks, get back 'ere" the old man in black scolded the dog. In complete defiance the dog went up to Selene and rubbed against her leg and looked up at her while wagging his tail.

"Some protection you are, makin' friends with whoe'er," the old man in black said. Selene crouched down to Sticks and held his head between her hands. "Sticks is a good judge of souls," Karon remarked.

Selene said "Thank you" and the dog left and returned to the boat.

The old ferryman pushed off from the bottom of the lake, kicking up some muck into swirls in the water. The aluminum platform slowly translated away from the dock, and began to disappear into the mist. Soon all that could be seen was a dark figure pushing along with long strokes in the fog. Before long he was gone and the night had fully set in.

Samson felt as if they had crossed into a different realm. They walked along the creaky planks of the dock onto a shore covered with a dense thicket of small trees and vines. A narrow, moribund path that had only been taken by a few, cut into the thicket from dock.

Selene went first into the thicket and disappeared. Samson paused. The entangled red coral vines inside his soul seemed to harden against the cool night wind.

The two walked until they distanced themselves from the lake. There they made camp in a small opening in the thick foliage. It felt very different from the forest they had traversed before the lake. The stars and moon hid behind the surrounding foliage. They could hear small creatures scurrying around them in the brush. They soon fell asleep for it had been a long day.

Samson immersed into a deep dream. *He was in the belly of steel ship that had sunken to the bottom of the ocean. Air had been trapped inside the hull, but it was thick and humid. Rust on the vessel appeared to spread across the surfaces at an accelerated rate. The pressure* from the water pushed and caused the riveted sheets of metal between large beams to flex and bulge.

He went to a porthole and recognized the crimson coral surrounding the ship. He wasn't one to panic, but he systematically evaluated the situation. The air was hot in the cavity and sweat stung his eyes. Seawater began to spew through holes in the hull. He wondered how this ship had sunk, and why was he inside the beast?

A porous wooden chest with rusted hinges lay in the shadows ahead of him. He crept to it and creaked open the lid. It revealed only one item, a small blue glass cube. The smooth sides and straight edges of the cube contrasted with the splintering wood. A beam of light found the cube and broke into a spectrum that colored his skin and mind.

Suddenly, his legs weakened and began to give way. The sea water enlarged the holes in the metal. He found a ladder that lead to a hatch to the top deck. That was it! He must free himself from this vessel of a lost age. The pressure of the sea compressed his lungs as the water inched up his body. He staggered to the ladder and pulled himself to the hatch. His calloused hands gripped the rusted metal wheel and tried to turn it. It did not move. The water rose faster and now climbed up the ladder and past his legs. He gasped. Maybe this was the tomb he had built around himself? Maybe this was his fate? No, he had left the entanglement and freed himself. He had survived without the metal machines of the world. This one would succumb to his will.

He grasped the wheel and threw all of his weight into it. Something creaked within and slowly the hatch popped open and knocked him off the ladder. Soon the hull was full of water and he swam toward the hatch, which also released a bright light into the cavity. He looked back at the cube in the chest as it sparkled and digested this light. Then the rising water churned around the chest's lid and thumped it shut. Once outside, his will broke. Above and to every side were the abrasive fingers of the red coral. The surface of the ocean rippled in the moonlight above the coral.

His muscles went limp, and he floated up to the corral. The currents of the water began to drag him back and forth against the red coral. His blood dyed the water to the color of the coral. He began to dissipate into the ocean. He was ready to join it. He closed his eyes and allowed the process to continue.

A bright glow drove through Samson's eyelids and his degradation was interrupted. The coral began to vibrate unnaturally. He was forced to open his eyes. The glow of the moon was gaining intensity and the coral began to tremble and crack. Soon fragments of coral began to detach and wobble to the ocean floor. His body dislodged from the red fingers as their rough textures lost their foundations. They scrapped and clawed at his ribs as he floated past them toward the moonlight, shimmering above.

Soon he was at the surface, even though his skin was fragmented.

He gasped the cool but humid air and slowly opened his eyes. Above him was Selene peering down at him with the thicket covering the sky behind her. His skin still felt as if it had been torn and cut, but he knew it wasn't.

"I must have been dreaming," he said. She shook her head in dismay. "Is it close to morning?" She nodded in reply.

No more words were spoken as they gathered themselves, ate a quick breakfast, and continued on their way. The sunlight soon started to trickle between the still thick foliage. The sunrise could not be seen behind it, but its warmth could be felt.

They walked and the foliage opened. They came upon an abrupt ledge that they actually had to climb up using exposed roots. Samson lost his footing on loose soil a few times, but Selene climbed up with the agility of a cat. Soon they were on top of the ledge and could see an open landscape of old pecan groves before them.

The pecans were no longer on the trees, but instead covered the ground in shells around the base of each tree. Squirrels and other critters had eaten or stored much of the production for the coming winter. In a few spots, young trees had sprouted from nuts that had succeeded. These trees were recognizable because they were smaller and broke the geometry of the evenly spaced rows go on and on into the distance. In this matrix of trees, a few of the original pecan trees had also died, and in some cases all that remained was a decaying stump.

The farmers here had long ago flattened the ground as best as they could, and also built straight canals to irrigate the groves. Ledges separated the land into terraces in the distance.

Samson felt different, and somehow still weakened by the dream from the night before. This was not like him. Nonetheless, he fought through it. The pecan trees were in the process of losing their leaves and did not provide much shade. Each step felt heavier than the last, but he forced his legs to keep moving.

He grew hungry, which maybe explained how he felt, so he pulled an apple from his pack. It looked full and perfectly intact. He ate it, but it did not end his hunger, and made him a little sick. He still fought on.

He grabbed another apple, and quickly ate it. It felt as though the apple had just fallen into an empty pit in his stomach. It never landed and he never felt it's mass. He realized that he should stop or he would race through his rations. For a moment he considered if he was still in a dream.

Selene seemed untouched by these trials and walked easily ahead of him. She crossed each canal and ledge with ease. He was a little envious of her youth.

They continued past line after line of aging pecan trees. Viewing the grove from the side, the patterns aligned and shifted as their perspectives changed on each row. At times a row would be aligned and each trunk would join into a single long being into the horizon. At other times the diagonal geometries would fall into place and reveal multiple symmetries.

Their footsteps often cracked the shells of empty pecans. For some reason this reminded him of the skulls in the pit. Time, geology, and perhaps other footsteps would crack those domes as well. Would those footsteps be those of humans, animal hooves, metal machine caterpillar treads, or something else?

The pecan groves came to an end, and the sun began to beat down with the final fury of summer. Ahead, where the trees ended was land that had once been cut clear, but now young wild trees and foliage were building a new forest. He wondered if his employer from before the Fall had ever rejuvenated this land using quantum entanglement. This evolving landscape was thick with bushes and smaller plants, similar to the thicket they had entered near the lake, but with much more variety in the species. This regeneration phase was coming to an end though and several larger trees had begun to dominate and change the land close to them. In another decade, this might be a young forest with trees reaching taller and clearing the land below with their shade and fallen leaves.

The heat seemed to be getting stronger. All the clouds had burnt away and the sun glowed without any restraint. He had removed his jacket and hooked it on his pack. Was this summer's last gasp before the onset of winter?

Samson had always preferred the heat of summer to the cold of winter, even before the Fall. Working outside in the summer sun always seemed to give him a feeling of being cleansed. When every pore of your skin released salt and toxins, drinking water seemed to purify your flesh. This same feeling began to permeate through him now. His weakened legs strengthened again.

Samson started to smell a faint hint of smoke in the air. He scanned the horizon in all directions looking for a gray plume. If it was manmade, he would want to avoid it, and if it was the start of an untamed wild fire, they should be even more careful. The boundaries of such a fire could spread around them quickly and trap them.

Selene smelled the smoke too and paused ahead. She was facing away from him and toward the regenerating forest. He walked up next to her and looked at her face. A few tear streaks were drying on her pale cheeks. Perhaps the scent of flames had reminded her of the burnt out house back in the town? He was not very good at handling these types of moments and struggled to find the words. He paused and listened to the wind weave between the tree branches.

The smoke seemed to be thickening. Selene remained indifferent. The wind flowed steadily from the west. He looked again into the wind for any sign of the source fire. Several wide plumes rose in the air, but he wasn't sure if the smoke dissipated from one controlled burn or multiple uncontained flames.

Selene stood staring into the regenerating forest. Samson tapped her on the shoulder, but received no response. The ghosts of that burnt out house must still be speaking to her through the smoke. Samson wondered how long it had been since the fire consumed fabric, clothes, paper, and the wooden frame of her family. Had it just been an accident? How did she escape, but the others did not? The scent awoke him again from his thoughts. It did not matter to him what had happened.

"I think we should move on," he suggested without any response.

Well, if she wasn't going to listen, he needed to find out more about this fire. A few rows of pecan trees remained between them and the regenerating forest, and one of them looked like it might be climbable by an old, but fit man. It had a large trunk that had grown tilted toward one side, almost as if a persistent wind had molded it, but the lean was not due to the wind. He realized that the entire last row of pecan trees were all tilted toward the regenerating forest. They had all grown that way to spread to the uncontested light. They had grown to capture more of the sun and open sky. The pecan trees were older than the regenerating forest so that when they were rapidly growing saplings, the field was still cultivated, and without any competition to the grand pecan trees.

Samson carefully climbed up a slanted tree using his boots to push, and his hands to guide. Once above the height of the regenerating forest, the source of the smoke was apparent. These plumes did not emanate from a controlled fire. In the distance, a line of flames spread quickly and closed in faster than anticipated. He quickly slid down the trunk of the tree, but landed hard on the ground and twisted his ankle.

Samson groaned a little from the hard landing. This got Selene's attention for some reason. He said, "We need to move, **now**." Selene nodded in agreement and began walking.

They continued south, parallel to the line of fire, but Samson's ankle slowed him from his usual pace. He leaned on the hoe he had taken from the giant store. The smoke began to grow thicker as well. It started to sting their eyes.

He thought about the situation he had brought upon himself. This entangling girl really had brought him into something like hell. He should never have allowed this.

Now he was in a hopeless orbit and had little choice but to follow.

Selene walked on, as if she was now impervious to the smoke, the heat, and this trial testing them both. Samson however could barely keep up. He felt like he was walking on a wooden peg leg. He struggled to keep her in sight, especially since the smoke was growing thicker. Her silhouette was barely visible, just 20 feet ahead. Perhaps he should not try. Perhaps this was the time to return to his own concerns and ways. Perhaps this smoke could cut any connection. Without much thought, his legs slowed.

The earthy fumes of burning forest, and pecan trees, filled Samson's lungs. He became lightheaded and staggered as he walked. His eyes were watering and restricting his sight even more. Sweat had soaked his clothing, but now he felt dehydrated. He stopped and took out his water jug. Was this one he had boiled? He could not remember and did not care.

Perhaps this was the time to stop his journey and rest. He found a tree and sat down with his back against it. He closed his eyes. It felt good to shield them from the smoke. He pressed the jug of water against his lips and took a long drink. Some water splashed out and dripped down his cheeks and chin. He began to mumble to himself something he had written in his mind long ago. His lips moved only slightly:

"Waves of flame
lap the beach
and remove
the impurities
of the smoky boundary
to be consumed
by the combustion
of the ocean."

The words repeated over and over, helplessly.

Chapter 9: The Hive

The toe of a boot kicked against Samson's arm, and then water splashed against his face. He awoke from the short absence. The nearby flames were cooking his legs.

"Get up! I cannot carry you."

Whose voice was that? He opened his eyes. Selene had spoken. Although her voice was still that of a child, it had the strength of gravity. He nodded in agreement. The flames were just feet away and some licked the mended soles of his old boots. He pushed himself against the garden hoe and lifted himself up against the tree. He was now wet with sweat and water, but his face was cleansed. He pulled the collar of his jacket over his mouth to filter the smoke.

Selene and Samson retreated away from the fire in a direction perpendicular to its boundary. Selene turned toward a field and a wide creek that might halt the fire. Samson followed.

Soon they had left the trees as their wood was catching fire behind them. Arriving at the creek, Selene leapt into the water without hesitation. Only a few feet deep, and she quickly waded across the creek.

Samson's ankle buckled on the muddy bank and he fell into the water. It felt purifying as it flowed past the curves and gaps of his body. The soot from the smoke was carried away, along with a history of mud and dirt. He lapped some of the water into his mouth. It tasted of the earth and its gritty fertility. The water renewed his body and mind, but the flames still taunted him. He sat up and looked toward the regenerating forest. His hair was wet and now draped over his eyes.

The flames finally stopped or at least decelerated at the forest's edge. The flames had consumed much of the brush and foliage below the trees, although some of the smaller ends of the branches and leaves had also burned. He knew they were still alive however. This fire could prove to be merely a step toward the forest maturing. With less competition, the trees would grow and fill the sky with a thick canopy.

A surge of cool wind rushed against his back and he turned his body to head toward it. The heat of the day had evaporated enough water into the sky to collect and form into a thunderstorm. The towering clouds grew rapidly, leaving a dark shadow on the land below them.

Samson rose from the creek and trudged through the water toward the other bank with Selene. They both refilled their canteens with water. She too recognized the growing clouds above. They walked toward them though, into the wind, and away from the fire. The wind would push the fire back and the impending rain might end it.

The air began to cool and a wall of rain appeared ahead. The wall, made of virtual crystal straws climbing into the sky, started with a low hum, but the volume increased as the travelers' path came closer to the rain. A few droplets did arrive early, but most of them came suddenly as they entered the liquid curtain.

Samson did not bother to pull out his tarp to stay dry, since he was already soaked from the creek. Selene did take out a leather brimmed hat from her pack and fit it tight on her head.

The heavy rain absolved Samson further, and the red mud from the creek flowed off his body in channels that resembled blood. But now he was tired. The fire was behind them and he sought rest. Selene could also tell that the old man was ready to stop for the night. They found a slightly elevated area among some sturdy oaks that would not collect water.

The rain ended as fast as it had begun, but water still travelled across the ground in search of either a route or a resting place.

Samson and Selene took off their packs and found several relatively dry twigs below a protective layer of leaves to serve as kindling. Some fallen oak branches also provided them a good source of fuel for the night. Soon they had a warm fire going and were cooking a quick meal. The creek water was now being boiled on the fire. Selene revealed some hibiscus leaves that they used to make some tea.

Samson fastened his hammock taut between two medium sized tree trunks. Selene had a mat that she laid over some grass.

They both sat staring at the fire in silence.

"What were you reciting in the smoke?" Selene asked.

"So you decide to speak now?" He looked a little perplexed. Most times the words were forgotten to him once he said them, which is why he used to write them down. "I'm not even sure what I was saying. The fumes must have warped my mind."

"Whatever it was, it was beautiful."

The tides surrounding his inner reef of coral pulled in opposite directions from a retreating wind of defense and the rising face of the moon. Samson was stuck. He had not discussed the beauty of the world with anyone in a long time.

"It would have been a suitable death and an end to this," he said, revealing what came to his mind from the thrashing and swirling between the internal red fingers.

Selene smelled the controlled smoke of the fire and said something unusual. "You still have unburnt timbers in you, an ocean below you...and a voyage to continue."

Samson's eyes glistened with those words and the coral seemed to soften. He wondered where she had heard something like that, or if she had just then thought of those words. He looked at her and just nodded.

Soon they both had retreated to their bedding and fallen asleep.

The next day returned them to the usual routine, but the forest fire had driven them off his haphazard southerly course. They were soon walking through an older but balanced forest mixed with new and old trees. Samson's ankle was healing, but still remained rigid and swollen. He laced his boots tighter to help stabilize it.

The morning proceeded in silence. Samson wondered if Selene would ever speak again. The air was cool and crisp, in contrast to the heat of the day before. He wondered about what had happened in the pecan orchard. Why had every bit of food made no impact on his appetite, and had often left him even hungrier? Why had the heat devastated his mind and body to the point of dissolution? He had been through summer days that were much hotter before. He had been through times when food was scarce, and all he lived off were grubs.

Perhaps he had been sick with a virus or infected by bacteria? It had been a more tumultuous journey than his usual migrations south. Being temporarily captured by the crescents had still left a curve cut in his mind. Then meeting this girl had submerged the cut in stinging salt water. Maybe yesterday was his subconscious mind fighting to be heard?

Regardless of the cause, Samson's soul was cleansed. The sky was clear, the air was cool, and the sun warmed him, but differently than the day before. As he walked, he noticed animals making their final preparations for the arrival of winter.

The squirrels were out collecting nuts and storing them high in the crooks of the trees. The insects were also buzzing and searching for any flowers blooming. The wasps gathered around the uneaten fruit at the base of a pear tree. He watched them cut into the fruit with their mandibles and suck some of the juice into their inverted bodies.

The birds also were busy. Some still were flying south. Others had reached their destination and were building nests for the winter.

The leaves of the deciduous trees showed more glimpses of growing rust. With one deep cold snap they would complete their cycle and fall from the branches.

These were details of the world that sometimes Samson overlooked, but today saw vividly. Ahead, Selene was also enjoying the mechanisms of the world and seemed to be a part of them.

20 feet ahead, Selene paused. She looked around into the surrounding woods. He reached her and she covered her mouth to signal the need for silence. He, however, required no signal. He knew the importance of listening to sounds that could prove to be critically important. He also knew the importance of stealth when stalking prey.

Samson also looked around. He wondered what Selene had heard to cause her to try and tune in. Perhaps she had spotted a large animal that could be hunted for food, or it could be that Selene and Samson were the ones being hunted. There was always the chance that humans were nearby. Samson listened for any rustling leaves, or voices speaking beyond the mesh of branches. He heard nothing but the sounds of the forest alive.

Selene stopped moving her head and zeroed in on a direction. She walked toward it. Samson followed slowly. He brought out his slingshot, found a rock on the ground, and readied it in the leather pouch held by the elastic bands. His instincts engaged his senses and readied his muscles for quick actions.

Then he heard it, a faint buzzing, but not the kind heard from individual foraging insects. The sound was a chorus of thousands of bees emanating from a single point.

They found a hive of honey bees in a wounded oak tree. The hive had filled a large hollow in the center of the tree. Samson and Selene could see workers leaving and arriving with legs full of pollen. Samson knew what Selene had in mind.

They gathered wood from nearby and placed it near the tree but on the windward side. Samson lit some dry leaves in the middle of the branches with his new lighter from the superstore. Soon the fire matured and was feeding itself from the wood. Selene than placed some freshly fallen green leaves on top of the pile. They began to emit a thick plume of white smoke. The breeze blew the smoke up and around the oak tree, and into the hive. The buzzing began to quiet.

Selene and Samson both wore long sleeved jackets so their arms and torsos were covered. They also put on gloves they had for cold weather and for dealing with thorny plants and such. Selena took out a plastic parka and cut two holes in it. She wore the parka over her head and aligned the holes with her eyes.

They both peered carefully into the crevice of the tree that was at Selene's eye level. The hive was full of filled honey comb, as the bee's had prepared for winter. They could see the bees moving in intricate patterns of swirls and circles over the hexagonal comb. Each bee knew its job, and all of them were busy.

Samson thought about how human society had once sought to reach this apparent state of mechanical perfection, but never reached it and eventually failed. What if we had reached it? Were humans meant to follow such a defined structure of living? Perhaps it was for the better that we had not reached it. In the struggle to mold mankind to this goal, through laws, technology and social practices, he remembered a good portion of the population living an unhappy life. The life of that age gifted little individual reward or intimate fulfillment. Maybe it failed because man was not meant to fit into this kind of machinery as merely one of billions of cogs.

Bees, however, seemed crafted perfectly for this. At one time, before the Fall, their populations diminished due to an unidentified cause. Some farms had depended on the bees to fertilize their crops, so it seemed they lived in a symbiotic relationship. Some farms even maintained their own hives. However, the herbicides and insecticides used on many crops may have also waged a slow war on the bees. These bees were also limited to a singular diet not found in the wilderness. This might have affected their health and weakened them enough to leave them susceptible to parasites and illness. Now, in this age, without the enormous farms or the factories, the bees had flourished. Whatever the reason for the decline, the insect world now blossomed. Samson wondered if humans would eventually follow a similar rejuvenation.

When the smoke had appeared to lull the bees to sleep adequately, Selene went to work with her knife. She had brought a sharp and long kitchen knife from the house. She used the blade precisely and began to cut out large portions of the honey comb. They would gently shake off the bees or hold them closer to the smoke to drive them away. Samson placed the comb portions in some large magnolia tree leaves that he had found nearby. The bees stung them a few times, but not severely.

Samson peered over Selene's shoulder and beheld the larger queen on one of the combs, and signaled to Selene to leave it. It looked like that part of the comb also had a higher number of dark pupa growing inside the cells of the comb.

"Leave her and let them expand. The world can never have enough honey," Samson remarked.

Selene and Samson collected an ample amount of honey comb, but also left plenty for the bees. They then also completely stamped out the smoke generating fire. They did not want the fire to spread through the forest like the one had yesterday.

The two continued traveling for the rest of the day until the sun began to touch the treetops. They found a good camp area and setup. After a fire was glowing, they both relaxed and Selene took out two squares of cut honey comb. She handed one to Samson. The hexagons filled with gold illuminated in front of the fire.

They both bit into their portions. The honey was richly sweet. They just ate the honey and beeswax comb whole. Honey was a curious substance. It would not be contaminated by bacteria and was almost always safe to eat. Archeologists had even found honey in ancient Egyptian tombs that was still perfectly edible. Honey is anti-bacterial for several reasons. Honey contains almost no water and is also acidic. It also contains a small amount if hydrogen peroxide which kills bacteria. Perhaps this is why many ancient religions considered honey to be a divine material.

Samson certainly agreed at the moment, as the steadily flowing sugar coated his tongue. The day before had felt like purgatory, and today he had arrived in a land of milk and honey (except for the milk). He was beginning to change his mind about traveling with Selene. He was also at the moment grateful that he had not been consumed by the forest fire.

The sweet sugars seemed to both energize and loosen his mind. He leaned against a tree, eating honey, and letting himself be mesmerized by the fire. The words once again collected in his mind.

<blockquote>
The trials of life
purify the water to wine
and transform the blood
flowing from wounds
to honey
to heal them.
</blockquote>

Chapter 10: Metropolis

Selene and Samson traveled for several days over low rolling foothills, dense forest, and farmland reverting to wilderness. On a clear afternoon from a meadow atop a rotund hill they surveyed the landscape. Many houses and neighborhoods could be seen on the horizon—the beginning signs of an urban area.

The fog returned the next morning. Selene and Samson awoke next to a smoldering fire on an island in the clouds. The coming day concerned Samson, as he knew they would have to pass through the city. During some travels he would pass in a wide arc around the city.

"Perhaps we should head East and circle around the city?" Samson suggested one last time. Selene did not seem deterred and Samson knew that they could save time by going directly through. He also had no desire for unneeded confrontation.

As they walked, the suburbs began to grow out of the woods on asphalt road fingers. The first neighborhoods contained larger houses on spacious plots of land that were now mostly retaken by nature. As they proceeded, the distance between houses decreased until walls were only a few yards apart. They could tell that some of the houses were inhabited, but others had been almost completely consumed by vines and the elements of weather and time. They had not yet seen any other people, but Samson knew they were there, probably hiding from the strangers appearing on their roads.

Samson hated roads, and normally did not want to follow them, but the houses and buildings were so close together that it was also risky to navigate between them. The roads were also littered with rusting cars and trucks. Some had been wrecked and some were just left. A few cars had crashed into, and breached, the walls of houses.

Briefly, two other people emerged on the road between symmetric houses far ahead. The people must have seen them as well, and quickly veered off the road and out of sight.

Samson and Selene traveled through once illuminated commercial areas, with many rotting out store and restaurant signs. The roads were lined with the shells of restaurants that had celebrated the speed at which they could produce food. Now they were still and vacant.

The city became denser and denser, until tall multi-story buildings enclosed them on all sides. Electric lamps lined the streets, but had not glowed for decades. Office buildings once shining with crisp panes of glass in the sun, now were checkered with broken and missing windows. The density of metal vehicle carcasses also increased, almost so that the roads would have been impassable by any functioning vehicles.

Samson and Selene walked by the burnt out skeleton of the regional capital. Its Greek revival pillars still stood as a reminder of the rise and fall of many civilizations over thousands of years. The white spires were stained with the swirls of smoke that wrapped around them during the fire. They passed breathless law offices and toothless courthouses.

Everyplace was silent. Samson still remembered when these same streets were filled with people. Selene had never seen what had been, and could not be aware of the true emptiness. This was the only world she had ever known, and she lived in it with ease.

Then they walked past the relics of a university. The once pinnacle of learning and knowledge in the previous age was now mostly empty. What precision laboratory equipment still stood inside gathering dust on valves and electronics? What equations were still written on whiteboards waiting to be solved? Thousands of books were probably still yellowing in the library and offices. However, even before the Fall these tomes inside were only recognized by a few hundred people, and now had been completely forgotten.

The university campus, once manicured to perfection, now was a still, unkempt forest of old oak trees. Branches from storms laid sporadically on the cracking sidewalks and rough grass. Tarnished monuments to founders and athletes remained, but now memorialized a dead entity, rather than a thriving one.

Samson recognized the faults in these remnants of the age of entanglement. He did not need them, and no one else did either. These ruins were abandoned for life and survival. However, he knew of one structure ahead that had not been left to die. The wounded beast had been resurrected as a bloody terror, although in reality it differed little from previous iterations throughout history. He hoped they would walk pass it with little excitement.

They began to see more people among these ruins. These people however seemed at ease with Samson and Selene. They went about their business as they would on any other day. Some carried water, while others brought in the rewards of their latest hunt. Some tended gardens in open spaces and others mended the buildings they had chosen as homes.

The sun was dipping below the skyline of the surrounding buildings and the temperature was dropping.

They entered an area with an industrial visage. The beast began to emerge on the horizon. The monstrosity was a giant football stadium that loomed over the town. People here had filled much of the old structures with new stores and living places.

A few new structures had also risen, which could be recognized because they lacked the repetitive mass produced building supplies. The new buildings did not have tiles layering their roofs in perfect lines and rows. Their windows were not exact replications of each other. Their bricks had more imperfections, and variations in color, but still carried their load effectively. The new structures had very few purely decorative parts. Unlike the ornamental structures of the previous age, everything was functional and served a purpose.

Many people lined the streets now. Selene's eyes moved rapidly, straining to take it all in. This is where the survivors of this city must have re-centered. Dozens of people walked in the street, talking and looking at the goods on display at the stores. Store owners did their best at marketing their goods to the passersby. At first the stores had fruits, vegetables, and meats for sale.

A blacksmith with his gleaming metal tools hanging from the front of a store hammered away on a raw piece of glowing metal. He held it up every so often to check the shape of the work piece. Hanging were hammers, knives, cleaves, shovels, and other farming tools. One knife that caught Samson's eye looked weighty, but sleek. He felt a soul within the pounded metal and knew it to be a fierce tool. Its mirror finish reflected the blacksmith's fire. Samson ran his fingertip across the blade's sharp edge. The blacksmith gave a quick glance up just enough to tell Samson he was watching, so Samson left it and moved on.

In front of nearly every store the people had now lit fires in old steel oil barrels. They tossed their wood scraps and burnable trash into the barrels. In some places people gathered around the fires and warmed their hands.

Selene was also at another store and examining the goods. She was holding a candle, but the store had many other items such as soap, clothing and other textiles. They noticed each other both admiring the wares of the contrasting stores. Selene disappeared into the store and Samson lost track of her for a little while. One part of him distanced himself from any concern, but an island in his soul surrounded by a jagged reef shook.

A store on the left had the universal Red Cross symbol painted hastily on a wooden sign. Inside, the shelves held many bottles of medicines, some reconstituted from the remnants of before the Fall. Next to them, and marketed as equals, were herbal medicines. Purified oils and dried leaves sometimes proved to be the only viable remedy now.

Soon Samson and Selene were walking beneath the cupped concrete fingers of the old stadium. A portion of the electric lights looming on the metal towers illuminated the bowl. A combustion engine generator must have been thumping nearby since this was the only sign of electrical power they had seen.

The grade of the stores changed as they approached the stadium as well. A crowded store sold a wide range of fermented beverages. Beer, wine and distilled spirits in chalky opaque terra cotta jugs and wavy glass bottles lined the window ledges of the store. Recent cliental also loitered around the store, clearly still enjoying the effects of the products. Several had dropped their containers and left shards of imperfection on the ground.

Samson kept his gaze rigidly ahead and away from the drunk individuals. Intoxication like this he thought of as a grotesque form of entanglement. These individuals shared for these moments a world that no one else could currently see. While they disconnected from our world, they became ensnared by a warped realm. Nonetheless, a part of him also recognized the usefulness within it as well.

Another store offered a more substantial narcotic that several people were smoking through hastily constructed pipes. Some of the pipes were pieces of old plastic bottles fastened together with twine. The people loitering around this store were mostly sitting on the ground against walls and trees, while staring off into unknown visions.

A red light glowed from an establishment not far away. Consisting of a long hall of rooms, this building was a little larger than the others. The structure was lazily built, and gaps perforated the seams of the walls. On the street outside women posed without much, if anything, covering their flesh. Some had lathered themselves in oil, which glistened from the fires lining the street. Samson walked a healthy distance from the establishment, and quickened his pace a bit. In the past he might have been persuaded by the women, but with Selene in tow, he would not. Even if the decision was subconscious. He glanced back at Selene, who had seen the women, but did not seem curious or alarmed by them. Perhaps someone had already taught her about the nature of these places.

Soon they were past the brothel, and returned to a collection of stores similar to those they had seen before the red light. Across the street, the old black metal gate for the stadium still stood solid. Barred booths at the gate collected a fee for admittance, but also allowed for bets to be placed on the outcome of the sporting event. Suddenly, a roar of a thousand or so people erupted over the walls. One did not often hear the voices of that many people in unison in this age, and thus it was a peculiar sound. Selene seemed somewhat intrigued and paused to look up at the high crest of the concrete structure. Massive gray beams holding up the stadium leaned out from the middle of the stadium. The stadium once held a hundred thousand people, but now there weren't that many within hundreds of miles. Now the parallel rows of seats never even reached a tenth full. Despite this, it still housed a horrific spectacle. Samson had seen the game both before the Fall, and now after it. What it had lost in scale, it had regained in intensity and blood.

Inside, one could see where space had once been built for food and souvenir stands. Now most of them were empty, but a few had been opened for these condensed version of the games. They offered food, and additional entangling substances of intoxication.

No official monetary system provided a foundation for this economy, although the locals had adopted some ad hoc form of currency. At every store and establishment, bartering was often the most common method of payment. One could also sell their goods, such as kills from a hunt, or hand-crafted commodities, to a store for currency also accepted at other stores.

"Well I'll be damned!" said a familiar voice behind him. He placed his hand on his knife in an automatic response.

"It's the mysterious old man," the voice said again. Selene also heard it and stopped. Samson slowly turned around and recognized the man from the village, Elio, who had given him the crescent coins and then let him go. Elio was leaning against a stout motorcycle covered in corroding chrome. The dark haired woman who found Samson in the woods also stood, leaning, into Elio. Another unknown man was inspecting the bike.

Samson turned and began to walk away.

"Hold on," said Elio to the woman as he jogged toward Samson. "What's happened to you? You look different somehow from the old bear we pulled from the woods. Not quite as reserved and feral."

Samson looked up at Elio with a bit of contempt. Elio also appeared different. He looked dark, as if his soul had been injured. Elio wore a handmade leather vest and had a fresh tattoo of a black sun on his arm. The tattoo was coarse, but the imperfections seemed to enhance it. He was once the illuminating leader, but seemed to have tumbled into a new, independent role. A spark of hope still glowed within him. The connection between Elio and the dark, fierce woman was still strong.

It had been just over one cycle of the moon since they had met, and these two had changed in unsettling ways. When Samson had looked at Elio in the village, he peered into a young mirror image of himself. Now Elio had somehow progressed to the next age in Samson's life. The reflected image seemed to have grown closer to the one he held of himself in his mind.

"You don't look so great yourself,' Samson remarked.

Selene walked up next to Samson and glared at Elio. Elio noticed and showed a bit of surprise.

"You've grown soft," Elio remarked. Selene drew out her knife and held it straight at Elio.

"Maybe not, she seems good on her own," Elio said lifting up his palms.

The dark haired woman had now slid up to Elio's side. She also looked different, as if she had undergone the same transformation as Elio. She was still taut as always, but the strength was now motivated differently. She caressed Elio's shoulder and brought her eyes on Samson.

"Hmmm. The old man I found asleep in the woods, like Rip van Wrinkle. It was a rude awakening wasn't it?

Elio, we have no concern with him anymore. Let's go. He's found his own way without us." She said looking at Selene. Samson wondered what she meant by that, but was hoping that she could draw Elio away.

"Rho, we are in no hurry, but I will leave if they want us to," Elio said first looking at the dark haired woman, Rhodus, and then at Samson and Selene. It seemed like Elio was interested in helping them somehow.

"We need no help," Selene said in a few strong words. Samson also nodded in apparent agreement, but part of him also seemed to hope that somehow Selene would leave his side and accompany Elio and Rhodus. They could probably guide her through this life better than he could anyway.

Elio examined Samson and Selene, still peering over the extended blade of her knife. "Fine, I wish you both well," Elio said, moving his gaze back to Rhodus. He turned and put his hand on her shoulder. Rhodus looked at Samson and then Selene, and then toward the ground. Elio kissed her forehead and they both headed back to the motorcycle.

The red blood in Samson's branching veins receded. However, Selene still stared and examined them as they turned away. The black sun tattoo on Elio was fully exposed, but Rhodus had older tattoos on her shoulder blades, which had initially been covered when Samson first met her. On her left shoulder was a crescent, but on her right, was a small and simple image of a lighthouse with stripes running across its cylindrical base. Lines emitted from the top of the lighthouse representing light.

Samson and Selene both noticed the illuminating tattoo. It reminded him of the brochure he had found stashed within his plastic container hidden under the flat rock. Selene's stance softened.

"Wait," Selene said with compassion. "You can come with us, at least for a day or two." Samson groaned, but probably not loud enough for anyone to hear. Why had Selene done that?

Elio paused and looked at Rhodus. Rhodus seemed to nod in agreement. They both walked back to Samson and Selene. Selene had lowered the knife, but still held it tightly at her side. Elio and Rhodus stopped in front of Samson and Selene, but looked at them differently this time.

"So...where are we headed?" Elio said.

"First, out of the remains of this monstrous machine," commanded Samson, while pointing toward the south, and away from the dark stadium looming behind them.

Samson also took a look at the chrome motorcycle behind Elio and Rhodus, "And what about that shiny machine?"

"Well, we actually just sold it. The fuel is just too difficult to deal with, and we were thinking about staying here or nearby." replied Elio.

"I'm not sure," remarked Rhodus while glancing at the stadium and the brothel and other establishments behind them, "especially after seeing the insides of this monster."

Samson responded, "With the looks of you both, I thought you'd fit right in here." With that, Rhodus punched Samson in the jaw. He staggered back.

"I've been wanting to do that a while, and you just gave me a reason," said Rhodus, showing the same fiery gaze he saw when she found him in the woods.

Rhodus looked at Selene, and said, "Why are you with him?" Selene said nothing, but took Samson's arm and pulled him toward the direction he had pointed, and the two began to walk. Elio looked at them both, but he did not harbor the same questions as Rhodus. Did Elio see something in Samson, just as Selene did? Samson knew they saw something within him, but he did not see it within himself. The light did not leak easily from behind the protective barrier within him, but the barrier was slowly diminishing. Like a faltering earthen dam, erosion was slowly enlarging the leaking gaps.

Elio and Rhodus went to the bike and removed their clothing, tools, and what remained of their food rations from the saddle bags on the bike. They were able to use their clothing to carry somethings, but it was cumbersome. Elio and Rhodus left the bike with the man and quickened their pace to catch up with Selene and Samson.

"Let's stop at one of these supply stores and stock up on goods," Elio said as he walked toward a store similar to the ones Samson and Selene had seen earlier. Samson did not think they really needed it, but went along. They bought mostly dried food that would not perish quickly and fresh water. Elio and Rhodus bought packs that were more suitable for hiking, because before they had used the saddle bags on the bike. Samson traded in the garden hoe for dried peaches and other rations. Elio paid for a few things for Selene, such as a pair of refurbished hiking boots.

Soon they had packed the new supplies and headed out. Although they were tired, they did not stop until they were clear from the entangling city. Ahead, the horizon became fuzzy with the canopy of many trees. The moon was slowly rising, and as it did its light twinkled through the leaves and branches. The sight was beautiful, and Samson's mind wandered to a strange combination of images and words...

Water

concentrated through the gap

accelerates,

but the speed of light

remains constant

even as it sparkles,

in waves and particles,

through pinholes

in the night.

Chapter 11: Vines

The group awoke the next day on the outskirts of the city. They had opted to stay in a house secluded within a woodland area surrounded in the distance by a lattice of closely stacked houses. After a quick breakfast, they were soon headed south again.

The landscape changed from what it was before the city. The terrain flattened, and the types of trees constituting the forest changed. More oaks and trees that preferred moist lowland areas now governed the land.

They were still in the suburban areas of the metropolis and it would be many miles until they reached a region truly untouched by man. Samson noticed many vines climbing up the trees, competing with them and sometimes strangling them. He removed his knife and would cut the artery of the vines near the base of the tree as they passed.

Rhodus and Elio noticed this and asked him what he was doing. "I'm freeing them," he said.

"What if they don't need freeing?" remarked Rhodus.

"If they are anything like me, they do," replied Samson. He stopped at a large older maple tree that had been entwined by a thick vine for many years. The vine spiraled around the tree in a deep grove where the tree had grown around the vine. Every foot or so a leaf would extend from the vine. At the same point, the thickness of the vine decreased slightly. The symmetry was beautiful as the vine twisted all the way up the tree. From the ground one could not see where the vine ended high up in the tree. The top of the tree was full with leaves, but a portion of them were not its own.

He touched the smooth bark of the maple, and followed it around the trunk, but never crossing the vine.

"What if you kill the vine, and the rotting weight kills the tree?" said Elio. Selene too had gathered with them around this tree.

"Wouldn't you rather die free than live entangled within another's life forever?" said Samson.

"I don't know, I kind of like the company of others," said Rhodus, almost into Elio's ear while she leaned her body into him and moved her hand along his back.

"Sickness could take one and then take them both," commented Elio, "and yet lives are meant to be connected." Elio kissed Rhodus on the forehead. Samson was somewhat surprised by the first part of Elio's statement about the sickness of other people. Elio, as a leader, had cut his people away from the vines before, but where were they now?

"But what if the others are different from you? What if all they strive for is height and success, no matter the cost?" argued Samson. He knew they could not understand the wrappings of the wires and wavelengths of the previous age. Would man fall into that trap again?

Selene removed from her pack a shiny new knife. The glimmering blade was the one Samson had admired from in front of the blacksmith! She began to draw it back but then in one motion laid it between her hands and opened her palms toward Samson. He knew she had gotten this for him and now wanted him to use it.

Samson's strong, but wrinkled and weathered hands gripped the handle, crafted in a glossy varnished laminate of layered wood. He lifted the blade and with wise precision, brought the curved end down onto the vine, but without touching the surrounding maple. The vine loosened its grip, indicating that it had been severed, but it still remained on the tree. Sap soon bled from it and dripped onto the smooth maple bark below it. They all watched as slowly proceeding tracks flowed in streaks toward the ground.

Each of them touched the tree and left to return on the journey one by one. Samson knew this moment held importance, but it also brought questions.

They walked the rest of the day and stopped for the night in a clearing near a small pond. The frogs began to sing in a wall of sound as the sun dipped below the treeline. The ground was dry and they easily built a strong fire to light the night. They ate more of the preserved food bought from the store in the city. Some of the food was salty, and made sips of water taste pure in comparison. They were all quiet, watching glowing ashes float up toward the stars, but the silence did not last.

Elio looked at Samson, as if gathering his strength and thoughts before asking, "Did you bring the virus? I need to know."

Samson was perplexed. What virus? Rhodus explained, with contempt in her voice, "Soon after you left, people started falling ill. First it was the children. A fever stuck them quickly, and left them barely conscious. They died in their parents arms. And then their parents followed. The entire village is gone, except for a few of us.'" She looked down at the ground where she was moving dirt around with her bow. A tear tracked down from her eye and departed from her skin at the edge of her chin. The fluid fell to leave a crater in the dry dirt below.

Samson suddenly recalled the two children he had met before leaving the village. He touched his forehead where they had placed the crown of woven flowers. Those buds now lay decomposing at the edge of a stream far away.

Samson said, "I had no idea."

"You were the only outsider to enter the village for weeks. You must have been the reason." replied Elio.

Samson's coral protections, that had been dissipating, now surged back. "Perhaps your gods were mad at you?"

Rhodus shook her head in disgust. Elio was also disturbed by his response. Selene looked at Samson through the smoke. Her gaze was like a gravity balancing the weight on his soul. "Look, I am sorry if I had anything to do with it," Samson said staring into each of their eyes.

They all sat silent for a moment while the heat of the fire melted them. The distant past started to emerge in his mind, and it was the only thing he had to say.

"Actually, you are blaming me for the wrong tragedy. Has anyone ever talked to any of you about what happened...so long ago?"

"What? When humanity died? We've all heard this before," said Rhodus.

"You probably don't know what really happened. Before it happened, society and mankind, followed a convoluted structure. People are always the same, but the world was different then. We were all connected, but indirectly, through signals in the air, and wires. The world's problems were being solved by science. We had learned how to tie matter together...to link and control everything. The marionettes were tied to other puppets. No one really held the control bar, however. The tying thread was called quantum entanglement.

"Once anything was entangled with another, both could be controlled and altered. We could create food from rock, no matter how far apart the entangled matter was. In a place of too much sand, it could be changed to water, while the area with the water partially turned to sand. A hot farmland could be cooled, and winter could be shortened. The world could be balanced. The climate could be fixed, and controlled. But it all came with a cost. Everything became entangled. I saw what was happening to people and their entanglements to each other and technology, being physically enacted.

"It was expensive to use quantum entanglement and so even though all problems could be solved, not all were. It was commercialized. The commercialization did reduce the cost, but then the cat was out of the bag. Its use spread to many applications, and new ones were always being discovered. There was also a possibility of it being weaponized."

Selene seemed more interested than usual, and interrupted Samson, "I heard of this. Seems fantastic. I read that they called it quorting? It must have been great to live then."

Samson continued, "Yes, it went from 'quantum transportation,' to 'quanporting,' to 'quorting.'

They never could figure out how to transport life. Living things could be materialized, but something always seemed to be missing. They were no longer living, what arrived was just dead matter. Then something far worse..."

"The secret of life..." Elios blurted out. Rhodus leaned in closer to Elios as the night grew colder.

"But when everyone was worried about the name, and the profound possibilities, something was missed. Something far worse than just being unable to transfer life." Samson paused. Why was he telling them this? He wasn't sure, but some reservoir in him was full and was leaking out. He looked up at the ashes floating on the swirling turbulence of the heated night air above the fire.

"It's not clear to me what happened, but nothing regarding this life is. I've puzzled it in my head for all these years, and this is what I've come up with. We were all connected, but more than just through society and humanity. The food we were eating was sometimes entangled. By moving water around the world to control climate, we had tied it all together. Air even became entangled. And when all the 'quorted' objects broke, wore, or deteriorated, it became dust and dirt, from which crops grew.

"I ain't sure how much or how long or what foods or objects caused it, but our flesh had been hooked together by an invisible web. No one really noticed or seemed to care. Then something happened. Something flipped a switch in the universe. Maybe the hard-drive of the universe crashed from all the overwriting we'd done."

"The hard what?" Murmured Elio.

"Don't worry about it…maybe we had finally stuck holes and connected nature together in too many ways, that this was its way of resetting. When the switch flipped, that was the day."

"…when everyone fell…" murmured Selene.

"It happened quick, and because we depended on each other for so much in our daily lives, the result was even more catastrophic. People in the streets collapsed and crashed their vehicles. Workers collapsed and the machines they controlled eventually failed. Cities, once glowing bright enough to be seen from space, went dark. Aircraft fell from the skies. Fires burnt uncontrolled for weeks. The cities smelled of death. It must have been what the black plague of medieval times was like...but I won't call this the dark ages."

"Why not? That is what it is." Scowled Rhodus.

"The people that were gone, were gone and what mattered then were those that remained. Some immediately began to rebuild and cleanup. Others took advantage, and thwarted any renaissance. Some searched..." And Samson's throat creaked. The tide of the ocean within him surged, and gathered in his eyes.

Samson steadied himself and continued. "But all of them, every single one, had been untangled, and freed from the manmade system. The vines had been cut. The survivors were free."

"Free? How can you say such things? So many lives, lost. And for what?" said Elio.

"You don't know that is what happened. It is pure speculation," stated Rhodus.

Samson looked at them both, and sighed. "I may be wrong, but what else could explain it. Mankind, life even, has passed through transformative events before. This is a new age without entanglement. We are all truly free."

Rhodus looked at Elio as if to ask if he was going to respond to this. Elio smirked a little and looked up at the floating ashes while gathering his thoughts.

"See the ashes? They are connected to each other whether they like it or not. The currents from the fire direct them, and they are altered by the ashes themselves, even if they are lighter than a feather. If they touch, they might stick, and then their added mass might bring them back to earth.

"We are not truly free. Like animals we must still act to survive. We must hunt."

"That's your choice. Some chose not to," Samson replied.

"But there are still forces between the particles, there are forces between us," Elio argued, while he caressed Rhodus' inner thigh with his hand. She leaned into him in response.

Samson drew out his knife, looked each of their eyes, then to ground and said, "Here's the thing. I worked for a company that used quorting to rejuvenate farmland. So it's my fault. I am responsible for a tragedy beyond measure."

He said while pricking and drawing blood from his palm with his knife.

Selene pulled out several yellowed pieces of paper from an inner pocket in her jacket. She handed an old printed article to Samson, as he wiped the blood from his palm with his sleeve. He had seen the article before. A scientist at a national research laboratory had written it for a popular science magazine. The title was, "Entanglement: A Warning."

Samson nodded, and passed the article to Elio and Rhodus. A bit of his blood smeared onto it. He didn't notice, but folded below it was a brochure for a community on a green ocean. The brochure silently fell out onto the ground. They examined the quantum entanglement article almost as if they were reading an ancient religious text.

"He's right, but it's not his fault" insisted Selene.

"But that's not the point," added Samson. Samson took the article, crumpled it up, and tossed it into the fire. The old paper, and his blood, burnt quickly and soon sent ashes dancing together up into the night sky.

Elio and Rhodus were digesting this thought when Rhodus noticed the fallen brochure. She grabbed it and examined the pictures of cottages and a white lighthouse with thick red stripes. "Where did you get this?" she asked.

Selene answered, "Travelers left it. My parents, they saw it too, but we were happy where we were. I've never seen anywhere like that. Have you?"

"I was born there," replied Rhodus.

"I knew that's what the tattoo was for," exclaimed Selene, revealing a faint smile.

"It's an island. People gathered there to rebuild. It inspired my name. Rhodus is the goddess of the island of Rhodes."

Elio clearly already knew this and was not surprised by it. Selene's interest however was clearly sparked.

"Why did you leave?" asked Selene,

"Probably the same reason you're here with us. I wanted to see the world beyond the island. Only, I did not need a brochure or an old man."

"Rho!" scolded Elio. Samson also sent a rigid look toward her.

Rhodus seemed unscathed, "then I met Elio, and he reminded me of the island's leaders. They had a strong vision and followed through with it. So I stayed with Elio's group until..."

"And this age allowed it all," interrupted Samson with his final words of the night.

The others had nothing to rebut with. In silence, they all moved closer to the fire as the night air cooled.

"Let's go to the island," Selene finally said. The others responded with a silent agreement. Samson knew that now he himself had been entangled, but he accepted it. He felt a connection to these people that he had forgotten existed. Nonetheless, part of him also wanted to be sure that he could maintain his freedom.

"The island is also south from here," added Rhodus, "and I will take us there."

"Did you have children? Were they lost in the illness?" asked Selene.

"All the children...all of them in the village were also ours," answered Rhodus.

"I am sorry...for everything," Samson said. Selene gripped his shoulder. The others nodded in silence—showing their acceptance of his story and that it was in the past now.

Samson had exhausted himself. He had not talked or interacted with others this much in years. The others also seemed tired and they each made space to sleep at a comfortable distance from the glowing embers.

In what seemed like a minute later, Samson was awoken by animal sounds in the night. He listened closely to the repetitive noises. They were actually human. They were the sounds of Elio and Rhodus making love across the still glowing and crackling fire. Their moans were rhythmic and deeply primal. Their sounds naturally blended into the sounds of the dark forest. Elio was joining with Rhodus deep inside her and were connected by strong threads that fed each other. Samson thought about the vines wrapping around the trees and how eventually the tight wrappings forced a symbiotic relationship. The tree provided a path for the vine to reach the sunlight, and after growing stronger and into the tree, the tree could no longer stand on its own without the vine.

Samson wondered why Rhodus and Elio did not have a child of their own. Maybe their child died due to the illness. No, he would have been able to see indications of that, or they would have said something in that regard. Maybe they were just biologically unable to? Clearly they had a deep connection, and demonstrated the skills and desires required of a parent.

Perhaps Rhodus and Elio were Selene's future? Selene would be better off with two strong and energetic individuals that were capable of crafting a vision for the future, rather than an old man who had reduced to a wanderer, and was only a step above the status of an animal. With them Selene had a future, and the world had a future. Part of him hoped that this was the case, and that he could detach the vines that had already started to wrap around himself. He had done his part. He had brought Selene here, and she had seen the world beyond her secluded town. He was not sure what the other part of himself desired, because that part was still enclosed in a nest of red hardened aquatic vines. Still, the forest fire from a few days before, and the cleansing water of the creek, had started to penetrate and dissolve the lair within him. These thoughts collected and organized in his mind:

> Invisible vines
> grow from birth
> up legs
> in spirals
> and toward
> the lungs and heart.

Chapter 12: The Road

The next day began with cool air and a clear blue sky. The travelers all seemed to talk more this morning while cooking, eating, and packing up. The previous day had given them all a deeper understanding and respect of each other. Samson noticed how Rhodus and Selene were cooking breakfast together, with Rhodus even giving her suggestions and Selene receiving them.

Samson had burnt the last iteration of his walking stick in the fire on the previous night. Its blood stained ends emitted the smoke they inhaled and exhaled when they were speaking, and joining. He found a stick of cedar on the ground that had lost its bark but was still solid and was of the right length. Cedar was a little unusual to find here, but it was a valuable wood as it tended not to rot. He use the knife Selene had given him to remove some protruding branches and to sharpen the top end of it. As he cut pieces off, the medicinal like odor of the cedar spiced the air.

They were soon on their way south again. At least the new destination of the island was in the same general direction of Samson's natural compass. Since the Fall of the world, he had never set a specific destination, but just followed the forces of weather and nature. Setting a destination worried him a little. He had grabbed his pack first and headed out quickly so that the others were still following him. He knew he could continue his way for a while, as long as they were travelling in the general direction of the island. But later, when they would come closer to the destination, it would take control of their path and dictate each step. He worried about when that time would come, but maybe that would lead to an opportunity to detach himself from the others.

Like gravity, something pulled deep in him into orbit with the group. The force emanated from Selene and kept him from leaving on his own path. Was it that she felt like a daughter to him? It was so long ago since he had felt anything like that to compare to. No, his gut told him this was something else. She was very wise for her age, and seemed to show a wisdom perfectly suited for this time. She seemed to see him and understand who he was more than anyone he could recall. Samson was at odds with himself about her, although he would never reveal that to the others.

The quartet hiked steadily for several days, only stopping at night, or to locate food. Amid the forests, Selene would also circle around the group. Sometimes she followed the group, sometimes she walked side to side with someone, and sometime she showed her youth and agility by embarking ahead. Instead of making their way through the thick undisturbed foliage, they followed a path that had been worn into the soil.

At a moment when Selene was ahead, she suddenly stopped. Soon Samson saw why. In the distance the lines of a faded black asphalt road appeared between the trees. This was the first sign of a man made object they had seen since leaving the outskirts of the city.

Samson walked up the worn path next to Selene and stared with her at the flat road ahead where still nothing grew. "Yeah, this feels funny. Glad you stopped." Roads, they always gave him an uneasy feeling, especially one like this that cut through and divided a thick forest. This is where animals would be hit, in contrast to the many intersecting roads in the city. The fauna instinctively knew to stay away from the large entanglements of man, but the crossing of a narrow finger like this was unavoidable.

Samson envisioned how that one day this road, this wound on the land, would deteriorate and be digested once again by nature. An age ago engineers had layered the loose gravel and used asphalt to bond them together, with the aim of the layers resisting deterioration due to the weather and traffic. Eventually, the temperature changes, and other natural forces, would tear cracks in it and free the entrapped stones to the Earth.

In the time just after the Fall, Samson actually used to follow the straight paths of the roads more often. With time, he desired the impacts with other humans less and less, and obtained more of the skills necessary to travel 'off the grid' and live off the land. Now he was a nomad. However, there was one event that truly caused him to avoid roads altogether. He had lost his only previous companion through the years when crossing a road.

Samson still remembered her and what had happened. Her name was Helen. They had lived on the same path long enough to have grown together in function, but not long enough to be inseparable. Their connection arose through serendipity, but it was not love. At the time, he could not love. Maybe he had lost that ability forever. She seemed to like him though, despite everything he was. Their relationship was almost symbiotic, but she was much younger, and held deep desires and ambitions apart from him.

Then one day they came to a road. Two young men in a truck attempted to rob them, but he noticed an instant magnetic gaze form between one of the men and Helen. After the men had taken what little they had. The man looked at Helen and she did not look away. He held his hand out from their truck. She looked briefly back at Samson, and then grasped the man's hand and left. He never saw her again.

In the present, Samson and Selene still stared at the road behind the trees. Soon Elio and Rhodus joined them at their side.

"What are you worried about?" said Elio.

"A road means the possibility of people. Generally people are good, but the devious ones tend to plan their attack around these crossings."

"You are such a pessimist," commented Rhodus.

"After what has happened to you, maybe you should be as well," replied Samson.

"One way or another, we will have to cross it. I don't see or hear anything," said Elio. This drive and positivity is why Selene would be better off with them, Samson thought. She could not grow up in the world with a constant fear of it.

Elio and Rhodus marched ahead and neared the edge of the road. Samson and Selene followed close behind.

Samson had no problem relenting his leadership position in this case.

The two began to cross the road after carefully examining the scene. The road was divided into three lanes at this location, with a center lane meant for vehicle passing. Elio and Rhodus had reached the center lane when Samson and Selene stepped onto the asphalt.

Suddenly, an engine growled just beyond the edge of a dense thicket. Like a panther, a black muscle car lurched from the hidden position, its rear tires spitting dirt as it spun onto the road. Several arms hung out of the windows of the vehicle brandishing the barrels of glistening metal firearms.

"Run!" yelled Samson, but his warning was too late. The guns began to pop and fire at them. Most of the bullets and firearms now were either handmade or refurbished and had lost their precision, so several of the projectiles missed their mark.

A bullet burst Rho's knee and she fell to the ground. "Rho!" Screamed Elio. She was immobilized and blood spilled quickly from her severed leg were it met the ground. The dark car swung up next to her and an arm protruded from the window. With a long sword the arm slit her throat. The car continued past her and swung sideways across the road and came to a stop. Elio fell by her side, but she slipped away from the world quickly.

"No...not now," Elio murmured.

Soon three men emerged and rushed toward the others. Selene in a state of cool instinct notched her atlatl with a small spear and slung it with force. It lodged deep in the neck of one of the attackers and he fell, sliding on the ground.

A fourth man now emerged from the vehicle, also armed. He had been the driver.

Elio rose with a determined rage and pulled out a large knife as the men approached. One of the men held up a rifle toward Elio, but before he could fire Elio had sprinted across the hard surface and attacked. Samson had never seen such rage in Elio.

Samson quickly ran to woods near him and did not look back until he was 10 yards within. His boot hit a log and he fell sideways to the ground, with his sharpened walking stick by his side. He looked back and could see the road beyond the leaves. Selene, however, was gone. One of the attackers, a stout muscular man, with little hair on his head or face, was trudging through the woods. He peered directly at Samson from 5 yards away.

"Don't come no closer. I will only warn you once." warned Samson, as his hand searched for stones on the ground. Samson drew out his slingshot. All his coarse fingers found were clumps of dry dirt. He grabbed one in haste and launched a dirt clump at the man. It hit the man's stomach in a puff of dust.

"I saw you on the road. You're just an old man. Whatya gonna do to stop me? Give up." Remarked the attacker.

Samson grabbed another clump and dirt and aimed for the man's face. His aim was good. The clump exploded on the man's forehead and contaminated his eyes. The man growled in anger and grabbed his eyes. He began to shoot wildly in the direction of Samson. The metal bullets passed by and cracked into distant branches and tree trunks.

Samson searched his pockets and found a crescent cut coin. He placed it into the pouch of the slingshot and took the same aim. Again, his aim was good. The coin pierced the man's eye, broke his eye socket and lodged into his brain. The attacker fell limp to the ground with red blood flowing from his eye.

"Dumbass," Samson remarked.

After regaining his composure, Samson sat up and looked around toward the road. The scene had gone silent, with no signs of human life. The events had unfolded with lightning speed. He grabbed his walking stick of cedar. It had been scratched during the attack and its wounds scented the air.

"Selene! Elio!" he yelled several times, with the only response coming from several songbirds. Elio may have chased after the men in his rage and Selene had probably escaped deep into the forest. Samson returned to his feet and walked crouching toward the road. He slung his walking stick into his backpack so that he could hold the slingshot in one hand and pull back the rubber band with the other.

The man with a coin lodged in his eye lay motionless as Samson walked toward the road. A worn and crumpled, but colorful, folded bit of paper had fallen out of the man's pocket. Exposed on the paper were the red and white lines of the lighthouse on the island. The paper was the same brochure he had found under the flat rock and that Selene had revealed the night before! "Must have been planning his retirement," he mumbled to himself as he walked past the body.

He gazed through the branches at Rhodus' body lying in a reflective pool of crimson on the road. Her blood had begun to evaporate at the edges of the pool on the sun-baked asphalt. Samson looked carefully and could not see any of the other attackers. At the edge of the road he reached down and picked up a free stone from the asphalt and loaded his slingshot.

Samson carefully crossed to the center of the road and came close to the car. Water, whether from leakage or condensation, dripped slowly from the bottom of the car and onto the road.

He walked over next to Rhodus' body. She laid on her side like an island in a red lagoon. The island had rose long ago in the form of lava and steam, and now was returning to the depths. He had grown to respect her strength. "The world has lost part of its new foundation," he said to himself in his thoughts.

He looked to the edges of the forest around him. In one area across the road he noticed a trampled area of tall grass. Perhaps he could track whoever left the scene that way?

Samson left the road near the flattened grass and returned to the enclosure of the forest. The sounds of nature, which had been temporarily silenced by the attack, now began to return. Birds sang in the distance, and the tree leaves at the top if the forest canopy rustled from a soft breeze.

Whoever had left the road here was now probably running. Their tracks were large distances apart, indicating a long, forceful stride. He wondered if they were too far gone now to find.

He followed the tracks, but soon lost them on a dry, rocky area that collected no prints.

"Well, I guess that vine is cut," Samson thought to himself. This was not how he had expected to part ways, but in a way, it made it easier. Regardless, the coastline within him had changed with Rhodus' fall. He had seen how Elio loved her. His vision of Selene finding a mother and father figure had been shattered, but perhaps Elio could still guide Selene. He did not know if they were near each other and had left in the same direction though. He suspected that amid the chaos that they had left in different directions.

Samson continued searching, but also continuing in a direction toward the south, until dark came. He stopped in a clearing near to a dirty creek. Several trees, which may have been willows, drooped over the banks of the creek and came so close to caressing the churning water with its leaves.

He drudged through the process of making a fire while his stomach growled. He took some of the dried peaches he still had from the city and ate. The sounds of the forest in the daytime began to transition to the sounds of a forest in the night. Barred owls began to speak in the distance. Their hoots almost sounded like the cynical laughing of observers who had witnessed the day's events.

Samson's skin was a bark around a vessel that carried something no one had seen in decades, including himself. The vessel might as well had been empty. The vine that had been removed had already grown into his own being. It had grown around the reef and was causing it to crumble. When removed, it had ripped off with it some of the fierce red boundaries with it. Now his conscious and soul began to leak together in a poisonous slurry.

The river of his consciousness had been damned up and separated from the ocean for many years. Now the fresh water met the saltwater, and the life within it struggled to survive. Fish of the ocean cannot be suddenly thrown into the freshwater, as freshwater aquatic creatures cannot be released into the sea. Part of himself that had somehow survived this journey through fresh and saltwater, now shriveled up and died.

Samson recalled a time in his childhood when his father had released a fish he had caught into the fresh but chlorinated water of a concrete pool. The fish swam in sporadic frightened circles around the pool at first, before eventually slowing and dying.

Samson wept. He had lost the only attachments he had in this world. The only entanglements he had let grow.

He could only hope that Selene had escaped alive. He knew that she could take care of herself on her own, and would probably eventually find shelter. But what if one of the men's' bullets had found her? Even worse, what if they held her captive now? Men like that were capable of taking advantage of an outnumbered female.

Deep down he seemed to know that this was not the case. Nonetheless, she was gone, and in this world of extremely long mean paths between the impacts of men, he might never see her again. Perhaps he should have left her in that town. She would have lived and maybe eventually met someone else more suitable to the task.

And what was that task? Had he freed her from the empty town and the burnt shadows of her parents? Or had he also began to grow into and entangle her, poisoning a human born and adapt to this time of freedom? He sensed that she could live without any entanglement, as could he.

She had chosen the path with Samson. She had chosen to let their roots mingle and feed off of the same soil.

Samson looked toward the sky and at a thin crescent sliver of the moon. Even though the moon was wounded, it pulled on him. The pale invisible vines of gravity tugged relentlessly. The path was bringing him closer to the ocean, and he knew it would be a high tide there.

His mind released into a painful freedom. He thought about the darkness of that road and what it had done. Still, it was inevitable. The journey would have eventually brought this outcome. The road was an inanimate object that everyone must either cross or follow. In time, it has the same effect on us all. The words that he thought were darker than usual, but also more dense with truth. He almost thought about writing them down, but he had nothing to write with...

The road,

rough and hard,

abrasively caresses

the travelers of life,

and strips the youth

from their faces.

Chapter 13: Separated Tides

Low and high tide never meet. If they did, they would cancel each other out into mediocracy. Their phases continue to trade places relentlessly.

Samson awoke adrift on a small raft of logs that had been lashed together with green vines. He had been floating for so long that the salt water had begun to kill the vines in places. As long as they held, it did not matter.

He rolled over and his head hung over the crystal blue ocean water. Dark sleek shadows slithered through the water below and slowly circled around the raft. If he left the raft, there was no doubt that they would consume him.

He had once searched the seas of his mind for the island, with sails and a taut line. But now his structures were broken, and this bit of floating wood was all that remained. He followed the currents and winds without any control over the course. He was at ease with this and accepted it.

For days his flesh cooked and withered away on the raft. When it rained, he would open his mouth and drink as many droplets as possible. Soon all of the vines wrapped around the logs were dead and brown. Soon they would begin to turn brittle and the raft would fall apart.

Then one night the moon rose forcefully into the sky. Its strength caused the wind to shift and the tides to flow in a singular direction. His path was no longer random. The random motion of the world and all its matter seemed to suddenly become aligned, like an infinite collection of small compass magnets.

The new direction of the moon driven wind and currents was relentless. Water lapped steadily against the raft and splashed onto his skin. The water evaporated and left a layer of salt over him. The vines also loosened and the alignment of the logs began to skew and gaps opened between them. The creatures below began to swim at a more shallow depth, as if they knew the time to prey was coming closer.

Soon he could see through the cracks in the raft the ocean bottom also rise from the depths. Perhaps that meant the raft was floating toward dry land. As the water become shallow, it also warmed. Then the round heads of reefs began to speckle the ocean flower. They grew larger and became more loosely packed together. Smaller fish swam and lived in their protecting structures.

The large grey beasts soon left as the water became too shallow for them. Now only a smaller collection of predators awaited below. He was sure that in a feeding frenzy that they would prove just as deadly.

Then something familiar appeared. It was the dense crimson reef, with its sharp claws reaching up toward him. He looked down at his chest and could see the scars of the many times he had traversed this reef and was bloodied by it as the waves drug him across.

He had no fear of entering the water again, and painting it with his blood. These journeys had altered him, and life had a different meaning now. The reef did not look as formidable as it had because it also now appeared wounded. Many of its fingers had been fractured. The fractured ends were still sharp though and might even cut flesh more easily, Portions of the reef had even died and turned white. Under the swirl of the waves, they would eventually turn to sand.

The reef was close now and the remaining fingers began to graze and peal bark off of the logs of the raft. In the past, he had fought them and swam to the shore in a bloody mess. This time he was not sure if he wanted to resume that battle.

He rolled over on the raft and faced the sky. Even though day time, the moon was still visible in the sky. The sun was behind the partial cover of clouds and could not compete. The moon seemed to pulse and send deep vibrations down toward him.

His head began to throb as the pressure of the air beat down and the water rose. It bulged upward and carried the raft high above the red reef. He turned over and watched the reef pass peacefully below. Soon his raft had crossed the reef and reached the calm waters of the lagoon.

The pressure in the air abruptly changed and the water suddenly dropped; the raft dropped with it. Samson turned toward the reef and watched as the remained fingers rose out of the water. As they rose the intertwining structures of the reef began to crumble. They could not stand under their own weight in the air. The currents of the moving water also cut the coral at its base and began sweeping it out to sea.

The moon moved quickly across the sky now and was touching the horizon. Soon it would be out of sight.

The destruction of the reef happened so quickly, it reminded him of the old movies showing the progression of a nuclear explosions shock wave as it disintegrated every structure in its path. The reef was gone and reduced into sand in the deep ocean.

The water in the lagoon was now shallow. The tidal pull of the moon was in another direction on this world, far below the visible horizon. Samson sat up and dangled his feet into the warm water. He let the raft drift toward the shore until his feet touched the soft sand. He stood up and walked toward the beach.

On the beach was his family—his wife and children—enjoying a day at the beach as anyone would. They appeared to not have a care in the world. He shuffled his feet through the water toward them. Behind him the sand stirred up to fog the clear water of the lagoon. Small fish swarmed into the stirring sand to eat small crustaceans that had also been turned up.

One of the children, looked up from a beautifully detailed sand castle and saw him.

"Daddy!" she said as she came running toward him. When she arrived she wrapped her arms around his leg. He picked her up and held her close.

"My darling!" Samson exclaimed. "It has been so long since I've seen you...as more than just a vision."

The two other children, an older boy and a girl, soon noticed and also ran over and held his frail salty body tightly. They just stood there in the sun and enjoyed the reunion for a long while.

"We've been watching you daddy!" the older girl said. "You've found your way, thanks to the help of a friend. Trust in the tides, and the forces behind them. We are all a part of it." Samson looked down at her, and her beautiful face with hair driven wild by the island air and sea water. He knew what she meant, but this moment he could never have imagined. He had looked and waited for so long, it was when he truly found peace inside that he found them.

He walked over to the sand castle they had been sculpting. The granular fortress was unlike anything he had ever seen. The detail was crafted down to each grain of sand. Spires and staircases turned to the sky. Windows opened to vast hallways inside. A bridge crossed over a water filled moat and into a large door that looked like a creature's mouth. The angles did not look physically possible. Small surreal crosswalks were suspended between the towers. Balconies protruded sideways from towers and hung over the edges of the walls. He knew that sand could not support these kinds of structures, but this did not seem to defy his logic in this world.

"Do you like it?" said the youngest.

"Yes, it is amazing," he replied.

"The sand works so much better when you know the truth," explained the boy. "There are so many possibilities that we never recognized before. When you become part of it, it's easy."

"But as with everything, it will change and evolve, with the tides and the wind," said another voice. Samson looked behind him and saw his wife standing and staring. Her features were also sharp, and real. Every crease and wrinkle were mapped on her body as when he had last seen her. She came up to him and laid her arms on his shoulder. She kissed him passionately on his lips. Her saliva tasted pure and fundamental. Her body deformed up against his, and their curves followed each other's. Her essence warmed him.

She continued, "...but the beauty, the information, is never lost. You are not finished with sculpting your part of the entangled world."

"It is like a big knot that we gotta figure out," remarked the eldest girl.

"Do you remember fishing with us?" asked the boy. Samson let his memories return. He remembered teaching them how to bait their hooks, and to even tie hooks to the transparent fishing line. They would cast their lines into *the water. Inevitably however, a line would recoil and become tangled in the spindle of the fishing rod. Sometimes they would just become tangled in their own slack when stored in the closet.*

"I remember spending most of my time untangling everyone's lines," laughed Samson. Still, he could remember the most satisfying feeling of when a tangled knot was actually released and the line was straight and smooth.

"Hold onto that feeling," said the oldest girl.

However, in many cases the line was such a mess that he would give up and just cut out the tangle with a knife. He wondered how much fishing line was lost on those tangles.

"Remember to always tie good knots where they matter," said his youngest child. "A knot is kind of just like a tangle where you want it." She was right. These tangles weren't all bad, but one had to discern between which ones should be resolved, and which ones should be tightened and compressed. When one tightened a tangle into a solid knot, it also freed many of the loops and lines into something that could be given purpose.

"I think he gets it," said his wife, almost whispering into his ear with a moist breath. For a moment he recalled

her nibbling on it while they were alone and free of clothing.

"Stay open but focused," she said. The she took his hand gently and brought him to sit down on the sand smoothed flat by a previous high tide. The children continued their work on the castle.

His wife continued, "...but you know this is not all of reality, it is only a representation. The kids and I, this is not what we are, these are just the forms you held onto inside. Just as names are merely a label and do not define us. We are all so much more."

The castle was down closer to the water. The children used their little hands to sculpt, but they would finish each feature with a gentle breath that moved each grain of sand into what seemed like its perfect position.

"That looks perfect," he remarked.

"It is, but so is the beach, so is the sand on the ocean bottom, so is the path of our many footprints leading away," replied his son.

The sun soon began to near the horizon now as well. Adjacent to it, on the same horizon, the edge of the moon broke the horizon. Time progressed faster here, as the moon had already completed its travel across the opposite sky. The sky began changing from the familiar blue, to blends of orange and red. The beauty of the sunset needed no enhancement by the dream.

The moon rose farther and its hold strengthened. The water rose and was soon rushing over the walls of his children's castle. Shards of sand calved off the sides of the walls and slowly flattened into the beach. The bases of the towers narrowed, and soon they succumbed to the instability and fell. The castle was still a jagged lump of sand on the beach, but as the water lapped over and dissipated into it, its amplitude slowly fell. After a few larger waves crashed over it, all evidence of the castle was gone.

"But we knew it was there, so it was," remarked his eldest daughter.

They all sat next to the lagoon in the sand and watched as the water rose. They were interlocked and touching. Maybe he could spend eternity like this? But then the water started to lap against his toes. They began to tingle. As he looked down, his flesh was dissolving into sand and collapsing into the beach.

"It's OK. Just let it happen." said the youngest girl.

"Look," said his wife nodding her head in the direction behind them. One by one, other friends, family, parents, and even other lovers appeared and smiled at him. He was able to instantly recognize each of them. Some he had not seen in fifty years or more.

"We are connected, you, me and the children, but it is not exclusive. Everyone and everything is connected by the fishing lines...the vines. It is in the very matter, energy, and thought of everything...but you already knew that."

He held them close and said, "This is hard, I don't want to go back."

"Yes you do," his younger daughter said, while looking up at the blue-gray and perfectly round, moon.

He remembered Selene, a celestial soul now wandering the earth alone.

Samson relaxed and reached down and ran his fingers through the water as they dissolved away. He allowed himself to seep into the sand. It felt cool and soothing. As he joined with the beach, he could feel each of his children, his wife, and loved ones, where they touched the beach. The energy of their souls conducted naturally through the wet sand.

Samson's flesh continuously dissipated away and he appeared to sink into the beach. As it happened, he felt like he was joining with the fabric of the world. His knees drifted away into the grains as his elbows softened and broke into fragments.

The water began to lap against the skin of his torso. The wrinkles and moles smoothed and his skin appeared young for a moment, just before dissolving. His vital organs shutdown one by one, but it did not feel like death. This was more like going onto a different, but natural life support system.

His heart gave a final beat that did not seem to end, but just go on in a continuous reverberation. As the water began to cover his shoulders, he laid his head back into the sand. His mind and thoughts began to trail away into a network of water flowing between sand and shells.

As the water filled and covered his ears, the world did not become silent, but rather transformed. The water fed the sounds of the rhythmic patterns of existence, on many different frequencies, synchronizing for a moment and then trailing apart. It reminded him of an extremely complicated and beautiful piece of music that would reveal a new layer each time it was played. He concentrated on one part and listened to the gentle melody while another harmony rose. Soon he could hear everything, but the noise just mixed to a wall of sound.

The last part of him to descend into the sand were his eyes. As his eyes turned to grit, which was far different from sand entering them, all the figures around him seemed to glow brighter and brighter until the last thing he saw was fully saturated light. His final thoughts in the realm came to him before his very conscious dissipated into the granular medium:

Tides
to those who don't know the moon,
are relentlessly powerful.
Storms
without seeing the swirl of clouds on a map,
are terrifying.
Stars
free of defined orbits
illustrate the divine.

Chapter 14: Moss and Mist

Samson opened eyes to a sun rising over the trees locking him on land. Was it all just a dream? It definitely seemed like a dream, but it felt real in his soul. He suddenly realized that many memories he had hidden away were now exposed. The memories were both good and bad, like diamond and coal revealing themselves in a deep mine. They came rushing to him quickly, burning and sparkling in his mind. His childhood, spent exploring the world and himself with play, returned. He remembered giving his children hugs before sending them to school. He remembered vacations in bleached and splintering rental beach houses on the Gulf of Mexico. He remembered dinners and breakfasts at a worn wooden table with his family. He remembered planting a garden in the spring with his children that never produced a harvest that met their expectations.

Samson's mind was racing. "Damn. All these years. All these miles. All that was lost. What was it for? What have I done?" He rose from his sleeping bag and knelt as the morning fog still gripped him from all sides with cold hands. He tried to collect himself.

"Well, what now?" he thought. If Selene and Elio were still out there, they would certainly continue their path toward the island village with the lighthouse. Well, at least Selene would continue. With Rhodus gone, he was uncertain of what shape Elio was in. This was another step in Elio becoming more like himself, or at least who he was before all of this happened. Elio now followed a chaotic path as he had once, with no attachment to guide him. However, maybe he underestimated Elio's growing bond with Selene. He was beginning to overanalyze this. He needed to continue the path they had started as a group. That would be the most probable way for their paths to merge again.

What was he thinking? For a good part of several decades he had done his best to head in the opposite direction of everyone else. Maybe this was all a mistake? Maybe he should return to his old way of random motion as he had done before? If the universe wanted them to connect, it would bring them back together.

Then Samson remembered parts of the dream. The strength of the moon pulled hard and it crushed the fortress around his soul with the tides. He felt a familiar connection to it. Selene was also removing his barriers. On that beach, for a brief moment, he connected to the entirety of existence, and his life's journey had a clear meaning, even if at times it appeared random and directionless.

Samson looked to the sky and the expanding illumination of the east. Moving his gaze to the right of the sun, he chose his path.

Samson had traveled this land before. He knew the terrain would be changing soon to vast wetlands and coastal areas. They used to be called the Low country. The people here, even before the Fall, and during the age of entanglement were known to live a slower lifestyle. They seemed to talk a little slower, cook their food longer, and savor life a little more deeply. They also seemed more connected to the natural world. The wetlands contained estuaries that served as a catalyst for life. Samson was not raised here, but it reminded him of some places in Florida. Perhaps the people here were living closer to an existence unhindered by man's contortions. They led what is called a simple life.

As he continued, the elevation of the land lowered, and the air thickened with water. Soon the trees, especially the oaks, were carrying the weight of thick drapes of gray colored Spanish moss. The moss entangled in itself in large clumps of chaotic wire. When the French first explored this land they thought it looked like the beards of Spanish conquistadors. The Spaniards in response called it French hair. From those times a myth was conjured and passed along to later generations.

The story went like this, a Spanish conquistador bought a beautiful American native maiden. The legend said he traded a block of soap and a yard of braid for her. Was it a braid of hair or a chain of silver? Samson did not remember. It did not matter as love cannot be bought. The conquistador soon realized this and confined her to his homestead, like a wild bird in a cage. The maiden escaped the confinements of the European life and headed into a nearby swamp.

The conquistador came home from hunting and found his bird had flown free. He raced after her and tracked her into the thick swamp. He soon found her deep footprints in the composting mud. Ahead of him, in knee deep water, she trudged on. The hem of her white western dress was stained with black mud. She had already torn pieces of it off to free her motion and mimic the clothing she was used to wearing. She heard the sloshing of his boots and turned to see the man racing toward her. She raced to a large ancient live oak nearby and climbed it by following its crevices. She went high into the branches so he could not reach her from the ground. After scolding her in Spanish, he went after her up the tree. She turned out over one of large horizontal branches that oaks are known for. He made it to the branch and began to crawl out to her. She retreated into the outer limits of the branch. The branch dipped and rose as it stretched out over the swamp. The thinning amount of wood beneath them began to creak.

The branch broke. The maiden fell into the swamp, painting the remainder of her European attire in mud. However, the conquistador did not fall with her. She looked up and found his body hanging limp from his dark beard still entangled in the tree branches. His head hung to the side where he had broken his neck. Then the myth ends with a reminder of how to this day the conquistador's beard still decorates the branches of the trees in the low lying regions of the southern part of this continent.

Samson thought about this grim tale and stroked his white beard. There will be no hanging today he thought. That entangled beard saved the maiden, but killed the conquistador.

Ahead of Samson the thickness of the moss spread and created majestically intricate draperies on the trees.

They were beautiful in how they all intertwined. But the trees also looked like they were weeping, which also fit the story of the conquistador and maiden. But who were the trees weeping for, the conquistador or the maiden? Did the maiden ever find the way back to her tribe? Did she ever find true love? Maybe that was the true tragedy here.

Samson was growing to realize again that not all connections to people were detrimental. This understanding had been lost during and after the Fall. With so many families, friends and companions taken by the quantum entanglement, it was practically impossible to not have changed. But each individual changed differently. Some gave up all hope and withered away into another secondary casualty. Others lost their humanity, and became narcissistic conquerors of what remained. Samson had never lost hope, and held on to it for many years, until the reef around his soul grew thick enough to shut everything out. Perhaps this was a fault of many among his generation. The younger ones did not seem to suffer this infliction as much, but nonetheless, everyone was susceptible, as Elio had demonstrated. Not many of his age were left, and he recognized that the time for the next epoch of mankind had arrived. This was the time for the next generation to bloom and flourish, even if his never had the chance.

But were generations, and epochs of history, distinct or just smooth changes and fluctuations in mankind? Some events in history were transformative, and clearly caused the relentless transformations to accelerate. The Low country seemed more immune to this. Maybe this was because their entanglements were different? Perhaps instead of being entangled in the artificial creations of mankind, they were more entangled with nature and the fundamental universe?

Samson thought about the Native American from the myth as well. Although little sign of their people remained today and even during his lifetime before the Fall, from what he had read, they too relished the connections made with the natural world. He did not know it, but the people of this world had also begun to renew this connection. One could see it in Elio's people, that he had dubbed the crescents. Could mankind advance this time without losing its connection to that from which we came, or would the cycle inevitably repeat itself? Had we learned the lesson?

The natural world was governed by physics, and for all of written history we have tried to label and define it within the constructed frame of human experience. But we failed to capture it all, and we would never succeed. Science did advance and make progress, but the detail never seems to end. Einstein showed that Newton's Laws were not general, or universal. Time and again this evolution of understanding proved true. Perhaps nothing conjured by man is universal, and true without exception. This may sound grim, but this does not stifle our search, nor our creativity.

Samson noticed that the Spanish moss does not knot or spiral around the tree, but hangs loosely like a hand on a shoulder, and entangles only in itself. It is not a parasite, except that it adds weight to the tree. Just as the vines, it does not draw life from the tree, directly. Were we the moss on the tree of life? Was that our flaw? Instead of entangling within ourselves and others—the moss—we need to entangle into the tree, and the framework of the universe itself as well. Samson was not even sure if humans were capable of this, but this path through the marsh, and the canopy of leaves and moss, gave him hope.

Samson recalled a book he had read long ago. It seemed to recognize the need for both functionality and beauty. In the realm between art and science was where another boundary, another reef, had been built by the previous generations of mankind. The author had proposed that what connected them was an underlying ability of the human soul to judge what the author called 'quality.' Samson thought of quality now as the ease of how things fit together. The moss on the tree grew naturally and almost extended down as a part of the tree. Birds created nests in the tree that too followed its curves and knots, becoming a part of it, and not easy to discern from the tree and moss itself. But when man constructs a square bird house, even if made stronger and with noble intentions, it does not harmonize with the tree.

This same 'not fitting' of artificial objects, caused some to become uneasy with new technologies and the modern world. But that unease was paved over with manufactured entertainment. The same technology allowed for the creation, or rather the near replication of a vivid alternative world of videos, music, and games. The endless stream of entertainment was like a drug that controlled the symptoms of discontent, but did not cure the disease.

To improve our fit into the world, the author argued that this artificial barrier between beauty and functionality had to be destroyed. Samson saw it himself before the Fall. A drugged society, like an addicted person, must either be separated from the medicine, or the symptoms of the illness must become so severe that they can't be hidden. Was that what the Fall was? The universe's way of curing mankind? No, too much horror existed in this time for that. But then again, nature was full of gruesome horrors. These ideas themselves could be another idea that man had created, and Samson realized this.

Samson wasn't sure what of these ideas were true, or were merely more layers of fabrications. Still, they drew him in as he continued deeper into the dense lowlands, and the moss and leaves blocked out more of the sun.

This world now had forced its human inhabitants to connect art and science, and to practice them simultaneously. Survival required efficiency, and aesthetics were needed to maintain sanity. Bits of truth began to emerge from his thoughts, but he could not identify them among the tangled moss. These connections between art and science needed to be maintained, and maybe this was the positive side of entanglement that he had missed for all these years.

He continued walking and then briefly the moss covered oaks gave way to palmetto brush and even a few large palm trees. The sun reemerged from behind the foliage, still high above the horizon. The ground also dried and became sandy. He was a little more careful traversing the brush, as rattlesnakes were known to hide in it.

Soon the palmettos ended and the ground softened. Many oaks again slouched above, wearing the dense beards of moss. The underbrush was still thick, but began to disperse as the ground grew damp and the sunlight disappeared. He began to see scattered muddy puddles and the old trunks of cypress began to lift from the land in wide taut fingered bases to slender, but strong gray towers. Around the full grown trees were tall rounded cypress shoots, called knees. Many still had no leaves, but appeared only as fingers breathing above the shallow water. There was something timeless about cypress knees and the trees themselves. Their wood did not decay, even in these relentlessly damp conditions. At one time, the cypress wood was an expensive material. People would scour the swamp for cypress trees, and even knees, until few survived. They were a slow growing, regal tree, that took many years to grow into the ominous giants around him.

The moss also grew on the cypress trees, but decorated them differently than the oaks. As the oaks branches usually spread far out over the land, and even sometimes rejoined it, the cypress branches stayed much closer to the trunk. The Spanish moss looked more like a woman's long hair falling down upon her shoulders. "Perhaps this was the mythical native maiden's fate?" thought Samson.

The puddles began to join and grow as he walked and the land inevitably was covered by dark brackish water. He was wading through water at a depth that came half way up his calves. It would take forever to dry his boots out from this. Samson also knew that this was now alligator territory. Still, the water was shallow enough that he most likely did not have to worry about alligators large enough to prey on a man. But even in shallow water they could be found in large ponds in the mud that they had dug out. He also made sure to keep an eye out for large mounds of foliage that might be protecting alligator eggs.

Samson thought that he should perhaps take a different route, and paused. He scanned the horizon of endless cypress and glassy dark water. Every direction looked the same. He found no signs of dry land, or even deeper waters. Then an unusual shape caught his eye in the distance.

Samson could have missed the cabin because it did not have right angles like most structures, especially those still standing from the previous age. No, the cabin fit perfectly into its swamp surroundings. Its curves were gradual and organic, and with very few hard angles. The tilt of the palm and moss covered roof increased until it joined smoothly with a tall cypress tree at its center.

The small hut had a small stone opening to one side, from which smoke billowed slowly out. Samson's first thought came automatically—to head the other direction. But there was something warming about the little hut, and he was drawn to it. It was even possible, that Selene, or even Elio had found this place.

Samson lifted his feet through the mud and trudged toward the organic cabin. As he came closer, he realized that there were intermittent paths made of stones, islands of mud, and cypress knees that meandered from the cabin in several directions. He headed toward the closet one and lifted his feet onto the bits of dry land. It felt refreshing to pull his feet from the water. He followed the path to the cabin. His feet traversed it with ease, as the path was clearly fabricated for someone of much less stature.

Soon he reached the cabin. The structure was on a small island that also appeared to extend out with fingers in several directions. Some of the island may have actually been manmade and reclaimed from the swamp.

The cabin itself was almost a work of art. Sturdy logs served as the core supports, but in between were woven pieces of smaller branches, vines and leaves. Near the base it had been covered in mud, which was long dried and hardened. The handprints that made it could still be identified in many repeating patterns.

Over the doorway hung an opaque curtain of many animal skins. He did not see any apparent windows, but the structure was so filled with detail that there may have been holes from which one could peer out from.

Samson walked to the door, left his cedar walking stick leaning against the outer wall, lifted the curtain of skins, and walked in. There, sitting on a wood chair covered in soft furs and leather, an old woman reclined. She looked to have lived longer than even himself, but also possible was that she had not received the medical life extending care that he once had. She had many wrinkles, but they were in the right places, and he could make out a beautiful woman under the canvas of time. Her eyes were vivid and deep. They seemed to strike his body and see to his soul. If the reef around his being had not already crumbled, she would have been able to see through it regardless.

"I've been waitin' for you," she said in a matter of fact tone. Samson paused. "I seen you through the cypress and wondered how long it'd take for you to get here," she explained.

She held her gaze on him and studied every detail, from his bountiful and sovereign white hair, to his tattered and mended clothing. During a long moment of silence, Samson observed her and the surrounding enclosure. The skins of many animals, including beavers, snakes, and gators lined the walls. Several turtle shells acted as bowls, whose contents must have been very aromatic considering the smell of the place. The stench was a strong, but not bad. The air hinted of spices and other herbs that he could identify. Several sticks with beautiful hawk feathers tied to them stuck from the walls and ceiling. From the ceiling, the moss dripped down, as if the cabin were below the ground and they were roots.

On one side of the cabin was a smoldering fire. In the wet swamp and darkness, the flames comforted him. Two iron pots where brewing something over the fire. Several handmade candles made from beeswax also burnt slowly and left a sweet smell to the crowded air.

"Yuse been through a lot—heav'n and hell—maybe ev'n more than this ole' witch." She said, almost whispering.

She picked up one of the pots with an old rag, and used a ladle to serve some sort of stew into a wooden bowl that she gave to Samson. "Here, eat. This'll warm your flesh...and let's dry your boots next to da fire."

He lifted the hot stew to his lips and sipped it. The bone broth, maybe of alligator, slipped down his throat. The stew was very hearty and his body soaked it in. She then took an old clay jug from a corner, filled up a wooden cup and also handed it to Samson. "Here, drink. This will feed your soul." He sipped it. It was very sweet, like honey, but had a sharp bite of alcohol. It may have been mead, the fabled drink of the gods. He gave her a questioning look.

"What? You think I'm gonna to skin ya and eat ya after you pass out, don't chu? I ain't that kind of witch."

Soon he not only tasted the alcohol but its chemistry began to work on his mind and soul. The details of the cabin grew softer and more soothing now.

"Now, let's see. Who you be and where you come from? There's something different about chu, that f'sure. You possess an understandin' that most don't."

Samson's already aging vision grew more blurry, probably due to the sweet drink, but it warmed and calmed him, so he continued sipping. He also finished the stew and its stringy meat and vegetables.

"You also a quiet one aincha?" she remarked.

"Yes, most of the time. Thank you for the hospitality." He replied.

"I don't get ta see many visitors these days, and you seem to have a deep, calm soul. Yet, it's been through some kinda confinement and a recent release…I've not seen a man in what seems like years." She said eyeing him up and down.

"So no one's crossed here recently…no one younger?" Samson asked.

"Ahhh, you be searchin' for someun'. It's someun' close to you, at least as close as you'll allow anyone. But…it ain't a lover. That I can tell." She left her seat that she had seemed to have conformed around her through the damp aging of the swamp. She walked closer to him and stared into his eyes and at his lips.

"You have a lover? I don't think so. You be a loner, at least until recently." She was very close now, and her sweet breath surrounded him. She had been a stunning woman in her day, and still was. She was thin, but strong.

Her hair, was long, but unkempt, and puffs of it would float of from the other strands at other points. Samson's eyesight was blurring further, and her features began to soften. The deep darkness in her eyes entranced him, and their power strengthened as they talked.

"I've not had a man in a long time." She said as she began to stroke his arm and stomach. She worked on moving his clothing out of the way. She pushed her old robe to her sides and exposed her body to him, although the flesh was out of sight. Soon her warm flesh was on his. The soft parts of their bodies conformed to the hard parts of each other. Samson had not been this close to another human in a long time. He had to admit, it felt really good. The mead had left him in no condition to fight it, but he would not, even if he could.

She slid on him slowly and in the rhythm of nature. He followed her a little, but was too tired and inebriated to do so completely. This woman in the middle of the swamp brought him alive. He couldn't help but think that perhaps this is what happened to the maiden in the mythical origin of Spanish moss. She had made her own way in the world, and become closer to it than most humans. Now she shared that connection with him. His thoughts emptied except for a few words.

We entangle in ourselves,

knotted up for eternity,

until another runs their fingers

through our souls

and frees us

to swirl into them

and the world.

Chapter 15: The Garden

Samson opened his eyes from a deep sleep, rejuvenated and ready for a new day. He had fallen asleep in the comfortably large chair he had first sat in when he arrived, and the one on which the woman had straddled him.

Bedding swirled on the floor closer to the fire where she must have slept. The imprint of her curled body was still visible in the collection of animal furs and old fabric. The fire only smoldered now, but it appeared that the woman had boiled some kind of tea. Samson smelled it. It was definitely tea, but it he was not certain what kind. He could also detect other unusual spices and herbs. It reminded him of cinnamon and clove, but wasn't quite the same. He suspected the tea to be comprised of local botanicals found in the depths of the surrounding swamp.

An old, but clean, cup stood on a curved mantel above the hearth. An old wooden ladle was leaning against it as well. He took the ladle and with several dips filled the cup with the tea. He sipped it. The tea had a rich organic taste. It had also been sweetened with Tupelo swamp honey.

Sunlight seeped through the draped door that he had entered the night before and warmed his skin. Its energy soaked into his body. It called to him to exit the hut.

He lifted the streams of animal hide and lumbered outside. Facing away from hut the depths of the swamp seemed to surround in all directions. The eyes of several alligators gazed not far from the hut. They stood still and just watched him. The ground only continued for a few feet before it submerged into the murky, brackish water. He also noticed that the ground was more worn to the right, where a natural path had hardened between moss and small growths of grass. He followed it around the edge of the island.

The walls of the structure continued their organic patterns of mud, branches and a few rocks. Then as he turned around to the back he could see that the island expanded in an oval shape into the swamp. The extending land contained a small garden. Somehow, the woman had found an opening in the cypress trees that allowed free sunlight to energize the land. Tomato plants, pepper plants, string beans, squash, and a variety of others filled the garden. A boundary of wild flowers guarded the perimeter. And outside of that and into the swamp there appeared to be additional plants such as rice that grew.

The garden was planted densely together because there wasn't much land. Thin spiraling walking paths flowed from the center that allowed the garden to be tended. In the middle was a small circle of land that was currently occupied by the woman. She sat in silence, cross-legged and facing the swamp away from the cabin.

Overnight the air had cooled. The morning was invigorating and crisp. She wore a single gown over her body, but the neck opening extended down her back a little. The opening framed the handmade tattoo of a moon, surprising similar to what Elio had recently acquired. He did not dare to traverse the garden toward her and instead sat close to the cabin. He watched her spine bend as she breathed.

Samson sat and rested his back against the wall of the cabin, but was careful not to apply too much weight as to damage it. He sipped on his tea concoction. Puffs of fog slid quietly across the swamp and some of them began to dissipate with the coming heat of the day. They reminded him of thoughts in his mind that left and were never remembered again.

Then he noticed the mounds of two eyes just breaking the surface of the water and peering up at the woman from just beyond the edge of the garden. One of the eyes was actually just a scar remaining after it had been gouged out somehow. It looked like a rather large alligator, for he knew that you could judge the size by how far apart the eyes were. Was this reptile stalking the woman? He did not want to disturb the moment, but thought that he should warn her.

"Mam," Samson said in a conversational voice. She did not move a hair.

"Mam," he said projecting his voice with more vigor. Still no response.

"Mam!" he said loudly. She might have moved, but the alligator moved faster, but only turning quickly away. It's large tail splashed swamp water across the garden and the woman. It swam away quickly with several flicks of its thick, plated tail. She looked back, giving Samson a stern but humorous look.

"Stop harassing ole' Ouroboros!" she said rising and turning around in a smooth flowing motion. Samson noticed that the bottom hem of her robe was darkened by mud.

"I apologize. He looked hungry."

"Well, he ain't consumed me yet. Maybe when I die on my own he will. Welcome to my garden."

"What were you thinking about? Still considering boiling my bones in my own blood?"

"Ha! No, no, I actually wan't thinkin' about much at all. I was listenin'."

Samson instinctively paused and listened to the deep sounds of the swamp. Many bird songs and frog croaks could be heard, along with a few distant splashes of water.

"Not to the swamp, although it is a beauty. I's listenin' to the universe. Wanted to hear what it's a sayin' bout you."

Samson wasn't much for fortune tellers or seers. "I don't need any knowledge more than I have, and I can't pay you regardless," he said.

"Oh, you already paid," she said with a sensuous undertone. He knew what she was talking about.

"And you right, you don't need to know nothin' else, but you made me curious. Maybe I can still help. I think you do have a peculiar way to handle connections." She sat down again in her spot, but faced him. She signaled him to come closer. She dug her hands deep into the dark naturally composted soil of the swamp.

"See this. This is every'ting 'round us. This is conduit. This is the connectin' ether."

She then dug around two plants that looked like some kind of large edible root. She gently lifted them from the soil, but some other roots also clung to them from the surrounding soil. They were from other plants.

"Just like 'tis, we all entangled, it cannot be escaped, it tis the natural and spiritual law. No matta if you are stretchin' to the sky, at the surface of the ground, or diggin' deep into the dark soil. We cannot stop it. It just happens. Between us, humans, between us and the critters, us and plants, 'tween the plants and the soil, the plants and the sky, us and the soil, and the sky and the water.

See 'tis gap of soil between the plants over here? The roots are attracted to it, and will fill it with great vigor, 'cause it is the most fertile earth. And there is the decay, the degradation. The plants all eventually die and decompose back into the earth. And so 'tis cycle continue, and everything mixes and entangles into each other. But without the soil, the fundamental, there would be no roots, no shape. Every'ting define each other.

But I feel like I be preachin' ta the choir. Am I?" she said peering into Samson. Samson sipped on the honey sweetened tea. The deep sweetness of the swamp trailed past his tongue deep into his stomach.

The woman watched him sip and said, "That sweetness, thank goodness for them fuzzy bees. Some of the sweetness pro'lly came from 'tis here garden. And some of it come from them tupelo flowers out in da swamp. Those bees, we work together with each other. They fertilize my fruit and vegetables, and use the rest of the pollen for demselves. Everything, depends on and exists because of each other. Even ole' Ouroboros.

But there ain't no use in me tellin' you all this anyways, The truth of everything is untellable. There are no words that d' scribe it properly. You can draw lines around it by sayin' what it is not. But you are also most likely wrong. I can't tells you where ta go. Just go. Follow yourself. Listen to the music in everythin'.

Hold onto the nomad in you, and around chu. It may seem random to some, but it 'tis not. That is what made you close to getting sometin' right. Keep following the currents, the eddies, the waves in the air and water. You will find the way, we always do."

Samson gazed at her and seemed to show an agreement, but not by nodding. His appearance had changed. He had already known everything she had said, but hearing it was reassuring.

"Thank you," he said. Then he drank down the last swig of the tea and set the cup down on the ground near the cabin. He dug through his pockets and found one of the crescent coins. He tossed it gently to her. She caught it and held it up to a stream of light that had navigated through down to the garden. The shape of the moon glowed.

"Well, ain't that peculiar? I also thank you, it's been like sunlight seein' you. But never fret. We'll always be connected and always have been. You has a game to finish."

Samson knew this as well. He surveyed the swamp around him. It still looked nearly the same in all directions. A soft breeze pushed him in nearly the same direction he had been traveling before stopping at this island in the swamp. Another path of stones protruded from the water that lead in the same general direction.

He tightened his dried boots and gathered his pack and other things. He did not look back at the woman again, but felt her presence. His first step from the soil of the island to the rock was easy, but the stone rocked under his right foot, and he almost lost his balance. The rock then tilted forward and led him to move his left foot onto the next rock.

As he walked, the water swaying rhythmically beside him babbled. It was the alligator that the woman called Ouroboros. The reptile's yellow green stenopaic eyes followed him smoothly from rock to rock.

"What, you want to eat me now too?" Samson mumbled to himself. He continued for a little longer and the alligator continued to track him. Samson pointed his cedar walking stick at the large gator. The gator quickly lunged up and grabbed the stick, repositioned it in his jaws, and shattered it into several pieces.

The cedar fragments left their odor in the air. The taste of the cedar did not seem to please Ouroboros, and he thrashed to show his displeasure. Then as the gator turned to leave, it curved until its snout touched its tail. It reminded Samson of old pictures symbolizing the cycle of life he had seen from history books.

Soon Ouroboros was swimming away in a graceful wave motion powered by his thick tail. The chunks of cedar slowly drifted off into the swamp in different directions. Samson had somehow grown attached to this particular walking stick and was sad to see it go, but its break came in a useful act. Samson continued on his path and soon was walking on soggy land.

The swamp become more like a bog, and the land was soft and almost floating over the water below. When Samson stepped near a tree, the waves of the land would cause the tree to sway above.

Samson's thoughts also seemed to sway and search for solid land. He paused on the conversation with the woman by the garden. This idea of unrelenting entanglement was undeniable, and yet he now had more freedom than he had just a few days before. And it wasn't because the others were no longer with him. Perhaps the fault in the previous ages, was that man tried to control entanglement. Some truth existed in this, and he dove deeper. He thought of love, and how one cannot control something so fundamental. If you attempted to force the creation of love, it would most certainly backfire. He had seen this many times in his life and others. You just could not fake it.

Perhaps the quantum mechanics of entanglement were just so fundamental that by controlling it with force that the synthesized were bound to fall apart eventually. It seemed that in most cases, if you force a relationship between two things that doesn't fit, eventually that bond would fail, and the failure would fracture both entities. It failed like if someone tried to glue pieces of wood together whose curved surfaces did not conform. You could use clamps to force them into place, and fill all the gaps with glue. The formed object might seem to function adequately for a while, but once a crack formed, perhaps due to an impact or nick, it would grow quickly and the two pieces of wood would snap apart. The dried glue was often stronger than the wood itself, and so the split would not be through the seam, but into the wood. Each piece would pull off splinters and chunks of the other during the catastrophe.

The woman had said more than this though. She seemed to recognize the path he had followed. He had actually never given up, but had relinquished the false control of artificial paths. By following the flow, he was actually always closer to universal law than others. Before he talked to the woman, he was physically free, but sought to control his mental entanglement. Now he began to relinquish that control as well. That last opening of the reef around his soul eased his mind and let him connect with the world.

As he walked through the decaying swamp, his thoughts flowed easily on these things, while he still struggled to recall the details of the dream from a few nights before. Piece by piece, the important parts came to him, and he now seemed to understand. He could still help someone else. He could still help Selene. But it wasn't just a dark quest, it was almost a game, and his time would soon come. However, he could not complete his quest by searching, he would need to allow for external guidance.

He found the fallen limb of an old cypress to serve as a new walking stick. The wood of the cypress, a cousin to the cedar, also tended to resist decay. He carved the tip, but as always, perfect sharpness was impossible to achieve, so at some point, he just stopped. Just like a work of art, it would never be complete.

His mind was now clear. Not empty, but it felt light. During this he had reached the far edge of the swamp. The spongy ground had grown solid. When his feet hit hard soil, he recognized it and stopped to reflect.

He turned and gazed at the cypress and pockets of dark water. The woman's cabin was now far behind. Some patches of tupelo trees grew from the muck. They had no blooms, but their vitality was apparent. They had large bases that submerged into the shallow swamp water and drank it. The golden jewels of ragweed still bloomed, marking the end of summer. Even though the pollen from those yellow flowers often causes severe allergic reactions, their beauty was undeniable. He had a revelation. The swamp was not a place of decay, but a place of rebirth.

Looking out on the last parts of the swamp, a few words gathered in his mind.

We began

swimming in the mud

and then dried

to run on the land

and now

we learn to fly

on the air

to eventually

travel

without any substance

keeping us

a float.

Chapter 16: Orpheus

Samson walked while letting his mind drift. Thoughts travelled between Selene and the distant past. The woman in the swamp had also reminded him to listen, so he opened his senses to the surrounding wilderness. He always listened, you had to if you planned to survive. But now he tried to listen more deeply, and to enjoy the music of it all. Maybe that's really what she had meant. To immerse one's self into the surrounding world, one might be able to hear the undertows and guiding currents of the universe.

His steps followed the currents in the daze he was in. Was some of that sweet mead still intoxicating his system? He walked for several days like this; catching food when he needed, stopping every night to sleep. He almost returned to life like in the days before he had crossed the Crescents' village and met Selene.

Samson traversed areas of tall longleaf pines teetering up from dry sandy soil. The days were still growing cooler little by little. The night saw the largest drop in temperature, and he tended to wrap himself up a little more. This was also a drier time of year in this area. In contrast, the heat of summer would evaporate water in the lakes and ocean each day, resulting in afternoon thunderstorms that had often appeared on que every day. Weather and nature cycled almost predictably, until men of the age of entanglement began tinkering with it. They could move water and control temperatures to a certain degree. They had used quorting to move water from the humid south to other parts of the country to increase the size of farmable lands.

The water rarely stayed in the quorted to area long, as the natural cycles of the globe attempted to move it back to where it belonged. However, the industry became more and more ambitious and began quorting more and more water from one location to another. Eventually all that quorting of water did change the cycles of the climate. In some places people had even become used to the unnatural clockwork of these new entangled weather cycles.

All that water was then entangled with molecules scattered around the globe. Perhaps that water, and its presence in every type of food and drinking supply, had a big part in causing the Fall. It took many years after the Fall for the weather to return to its normal balance.

He now realized something else. To think that after all this time, and after everything had appeared to return to the natural order, that the particles were no longer entangled was a mistake. Everything is entangled, and always has been. He understood that now. Since all the matter and all the structuring began from the big bang, everything has been entangled. Every subatomic particle, every system, were entangled and always would be. However, it followed a natural order such that large quantities of matter did not change at what appeared to be random moments. Nonetheless, the matter in each object and therefore every living creature was entangled and changing continuously.

This all reminded Samson of the idea of alchemy, and how many centuries ago people had sworn they could change matter from one substance to another. The ultimate synthesized substance was of course gold. Maybe there was some truth to these observations? Maybe these were quantum entanglement anomalies? He doubted it, but in his current state of mind everything seemed possible.

The cry of a hawk brought Samson's mind back to his path through the woods. The sun was on its way toward the horizon and clouds were gathering above to make it seem darker and later in the day than it was. He could hear every chirp and every leaf rustle as animals scurried away. Then he heard something different, a musical note, but not from a bird. He at first did not react, because his mind was probably just playing tricks on him. Then the sequence of several notes rose faintly above the forest. They blended in perfectly with the sounds of nature.

Samson halted and turned his head slowly around to locate the source of the music. He found it in a direction almost due east to him. In the past, he would turn his course toward the opposite direction. Now, however, he wasn't sure. And the music was undeniably beautiful.

The guitar strings were plucked with a tenderness that conveyed sweet vibrations with each note, but the finger strikes were still strong enough to send the noise to signal out in all directions.

A voice also sang over the notes. He did not think that he had heard the words or the song before, but he recognized the voice. At first, he just stood stunned and closed his eyes to hear the music. His body swayed in the wind as it gusted against his back. He opened his eyes and began walking toward the song. The voice continued singing:

"You have no choice,
but to follow nature
toward her voice,
and her cure..."

The words travelled on the voice of a man, but it wasn't a deep voice, and it tapped into a deep vein of emotion. The vein was opening and spilling out the love and pain of the world.

"It's in her fruit
and the flesh
bringing pain to mute
an answer to a wish."

The music sent power to each stride, and he unconsciously stepped in rhythm. It slowly became louder and clearer.

"You can't resist
her ocean blue,
her morning mist,
she is your muse."

Samson finally caught a glimpse of something through the trees. The surfaces seen through the gaps in the leaves were rounded and worn, but still glossy white. Soon the fuselage of a jet airliner came into view. It must have crashed during the Fall. Only one section of the plane lay there, and the sections with the wings, and engines were nowhere to be seen. The cockpit stood still intact at one end of the fuselage, but the other end was cracked open like the open half of a broken egg.

As Samson walked closer, he could see a few people gathered around a fire near the open end of the fuselage. Facing him from across the fire was a round looking man strumming on an old guitar and singing. He had long hair that covered his eyes like Spanish moss as he looked below toward the guitar strings. The hollow fuselage acted like the body of a giant instrument, and the sound resonated out.

Another large muscled figure also faced him. His physical stature stood in contrast to the bard. His clothing had been torn and bloodied, but appeared to make up a color coordinated uniform with a number hastily painted on the front. The man wore a bandage around one eye.

An additional smaller figure faced away from him, wearing a hooded jacket that was much too large. It struck him that it could be Selene. What were the odds of finding another child out here?

The musician continued to play his guitar, but did not sing. He reverted to a classical guitar style where he plucked and resonated the individual strings. His fingers danced across the taut strings like the thin legs of a water strider over the shallow ripples of a creek.

Samson drew out the knife Selene had given him a few days before, just in case. The day was darkening and he thought he was still out of view of the figures. He crept slowly toward the camp and sought to ascertain the situation. If it was Selene, he could probably make his presence known and waltz in. However, what if Selene was not here of her own free will?

Samson crept closer and closer, exposing more of him from the leaves and tree trunks. The fire cast long shadows of the trees into the forest. The figures had an iron scaffold suspending a pot of some kind of stew over the fire. Its pleasantly appetizing essence dissipated into the forest air.

Samson closed in. Soon they would hear him breathing. His foot then cracked a small twig. The small figure turned its head. Selene! The old woman had advised him to follow the music, but he had not taken her statement literally. But here Selene was.

A line of cold metal suddenly pressed into a wrinkle across his throat. A strong voice said, "Don't move old man."

With this, Selene turned completely around and saw him. She didn't say a word, but left the log she was seated on and raced to him. With the knife stiff on his throat, she wrapped her arms around him tightly. The knife released from his throat and the man wielding it stepped back.

The guitar playing had stopped, and the musician said, "Now who is this?"

Selene replied, "He is the one I told you about. We have been calling him Samson, but I have a feeling that is not his name." Samson had almost gotten used to the name Elio had given him. After forgetting his identity for so long, it was easy to accept a new one.

"Samson is fine," he remarked. He had to admit, that at the moment he was just pleased to find Selene. Not that she could not take care of herself, but this felt like the right path to be on.

The musician leaned his guitar against the fuselage and stood up. He appeared to be approximately the same age as Samson. His guitar was like many other items of their age, repaired but functional. Splintered wood had been glued back in place, and duct tape covered a crack in the body.

"Please, join us," he said, gesturing to Samson to sit down next to the fire. "Folks have tended to call me 'O,' since…well…I never bothered to change my legal name, but that was my professional name."

Samson somehow recognized the round, but engulfing presence of this man. "You seem familiar," he said as he sat down.

The musician smiled and said "I don't get that very much anymore. Most who could remember those days are now gone. I was once a performer, a musician, really, a rock star, whatever you want to call it. You probably saw me in video, but I was never the most popular. I hung on some old ideas and did my best to keep them alive. I suppose that even now my job hasn't changed much. Now I suppose that I am more like some medieval minstrel…"

Samson could now remember. He actually enjoyed this man's music—that had been proliferated around the globe. "I remember you and your music. I actually liked to listen to it very much."

"Really? Yeah, I suppose it's possible. I used to travel around in one of these," He said as he tapped the jet airliner carcass just behind him. "I used to play to thousands…"

"Well, numbers don't matter anymore."

"Yes, that's true. So what's your story? I have to admit that it's good to see someone from those days," the musician asked.

"You seem to wish to be back in those days? It doesn't matter who I am. Honestly, I'm not sure if I remember anymore." Samson looked at the ever changing flames of the fire, and allowed the smoke to sting his eyes. "It's taken me this long, but I now realize, what really matters is now. Oh, and thank you for finding her."

"Find her? No, she found me, just like those two did, and now you" the musician said nodding to the two younger athletic men. Yes, a part of me misses those days. I was like a god. But I've also come to realize that it did not bring me deep satisfaction, or happiness...and now all that seems forgotten."

"Well, your skill, your musical light drew us here. You were a beacon back then, and you still are." Samson said. Selene must have seen the sincerity and nodded in approval. "That said, I'd enjoy hearing your art once again." Samson said as he walked to Selene, patted her on the shoulder and sat down.

"Very well," said O. He sat down and began checking the tuning on his guitar.

"Alright old man, sorry for the knife, maybe you'd like some stew?" said the man who had caught him from behind, and now sat opposite to him next to the other man who never left his seat. Samson turned to take a look at him. The torn and dirty jersey with crimson stains hung loosely on his athletic frame.

"You two had enough blood ball?" Samson remarked.

"So you know the game?"

"I've watched how it's continued to degrade over the years, but mostly I try to avoid it. Still, I suppose we all gotta find a way to get by. Whatya go by?"

"Well, we go by our professional names, mine's Nike, and that one-eyed fellow over there is Ares. He had a tough one, and yes, we're taking a break." While Nike was talking, he had filed an old metal bowl full of the stew that had been simmering above the fire.

"Here, it's an old family recipe," Nike said with a wink to Samson. Samson brought the whole bowl up to his lips a sucked some out from over the rim. The fluid was hearty, but did not have the best taste. It tasted as though they had cooked an animal that had been eating some bitter plants, or maybe they had added some wild herbs they had found in the forest. Nonetheless, it filled his stomach, and he was grateful.

"Thank you," Samson said. Samson knew that there was more to their story than that, but he wanted to talk to Selene. Without even looking in her direction, he said, "What happened?"

Selene brushed the hair away from her face and spoke, "I ran into the woods soon after those men attacked. One seemed to follow me, but I lost him fairly easy. I had run so fast I did not know where everyone else was, or how to get back. I did see Rho," she said while looking up with a sad questioning expression. She was asking him what happened to her. Samson just shook his head.

"I liked her," Selene said with a tremble in her voice, but still showing composure rarely seen in someone her age. "What of Elio?"

"I don't know. One of them was after me, but I saw Elio attack the other man with a rage rarely seen. When I returned to the car, everyone was gone, except for Rho. It was such a broken scene."

Selene looked in the fire and murmured, "I was really down and wandering in a daze, but then I heard O's music echoing through the forest. He is a kind soul. I've been here for several days."

O's fingers interrupted them and sent music out from the old wooden guitar once again. The soundwaves appeared to cause the smoke above the fire to dance. He wondered if the wild creatures appreciated these controlled vibrations, or if it was just some strange sound to them. Maybe seeing the musician had reminded Samson of one of his old songs from before the Fall, or maybe it was just serendipity, but the words sang mirrored Samson's thoughts.

"Does the bird,

whistling whirls,

find beauty

in her own song?

Does the lover

know the ache

that will come

in not too long?

Do they listen

to the others?

Do they gaze

at the unlike feathers?

I dream that they do.

I dream that we do."

Chapter 17: Blood and Leather

The strumming sounds of the guitar and a soft but resonating voice continued to blend into the wild sounds of the forest at night for several more songs. During this the others did not speak much, mostly because it would disrupt the beauty. But then O set down his beat up guitar and instead of singing, talked toward Samson, "You and I are like this old guitar. Our tones may not be as pure and vibrant as before, but we can still make music and maybe in a richer version. The imperfections, the duck tape repairing this hole, the worn points between the frets, the stretched strings, maybe they all add to the depth."

"Your evaluation sounds appealing, but I'd still take being young again. Being untarnished." Samson responded.

"But what would you give up by doing so? Anyway, I'm sure these youngsters don't want us talking about getting old all night."

Samson nodded in agreement. Rummaging through his pack he drew out yaupon leaves and brewed them in five cups provided by O.

"This is good. So this is one of the planes that came down during the Fall?" remarked Selene, sipping on the tea and looking at Samson. Was she comparing this to what he had said over other steaming cups and piles of burning wood?

"Yes, it looks like it," replied Samson as he handed the cups out.

Sipping on his tea, O also weighed in, "I think so too. When I found it, there were some remains of passengers and the pilots. So I began removing them and burying them properly. A good portion of them had strange distortions or growths on their bones. Actually, when I got to the pilots, they all had these unnatural formations. One of their skulls even had a jagged gap on the dome."

"It doesn't surprise me," said Samson.

"I explained your theory of quantum entanglement to them," added Selene.

"That going to happen again?" asked Ares, the stilled seated and injured athlete.

Samson replied, "Who knows? By definition, it is difficult to predict quantum events. But we can't live our lives worrying about something we cannot fix. However, as time goes on, I think it is less likely. You see, as the entangled atoms and molecules become more mixed up, it is much less likely. All of us, every part of us, is always entangled, but not in an artificially ordered manner…"

"Alright old man. We get the point. That's enough science for two beat up gladiators, Besides, Ares over there is the strategic mind between us." said Nike. Ares just shrugged his shoulders.

"So what's your real story here? I thought the coliseum lords treated the gladiators well...when you weren't playing?" asked Samson.

"Yes, but when you aren't winning, or are physically spent, your life is done to them. They don't have green pastures to allow their horses to spend their final days upon," Nike began. "

"Ares, Nike, those are Greek god names. Not Roman gladiators..."

"Yeah, the lords just name us, probably just picking out what sounds glorious. So Samson is it? Do you lose what strength you have if I cut your hair?"

Samson, running his fingers through his white wavy hair, answered, "Well, my strength is always fading. No modern medicine to keep me young anymore. But, someone gave me this name not too long ago."

O suddenly came to life, and spoke, "Samson, it is biblical, but it also means 'sun,' or sometimes 'as bright as the sun.' And interestingly, Selene is the goddess of the moon."

"Gee, thanks," Selene remarked looking at Samson.

"...and Selene is the sister of Helios, the God of the Sun." added Samson.

"Studying ancient mythology must be a past time of both your youths?" laughed Ares.

"Laughing are we, Ares? You must be feeling better?" said Nike.

"Perhaps. And we speak of Gods like we are them. Look around. This age is lost. If we are Gods, we are a diluted bloodline. Look how Olympus has degraded. Let it go. It is gone. We have no lightning to wield now. The magic is gone." With that Ares slipped off the log he was sitting on and brought himself to the ground, with his back against the bark. Samson noticed him wince has he moved.

Samson countered, "O and I lived in the time before. There never was any magic. None of us were ever Gods. Mankind has always been faulty, that is why the Fall happened...but the good in us, the bad, it all fits together."

O added, "I was probably as close as anyone came to being a God, at least in some aspects, but look at me now. I'm just a man, and an old one. It didn't help me when the foundations fell apart, but they were already cracking even before it happened. They always are."

Samson continued, "I've seen the worst. I've seen when the jet planes fell and opened gaps in walls, store windows and in society. What was left of the structure could not bear the load and collapsed. There was looting and chaos. Maybe it was nature retuning and balancing us. We were so skewed to one way of living, so dependent on the artificial mechanisms. We were not free.

"For a long time I did not see it, but humanity has survived and is restructuring. Maybe this time we will rise, but in a more natural...balanced direction. The mechanisms we built attempted to control nature and each other. The controls put tension on us and the social structure, until it all began to snap.

"But that does not mean we should do nothing. That is what I did for so long. We must keep moving, but don't force what direction is forward..."

Selene interrupted, "but you never stopped moving, sometimes getting lost is the only way to find the best path,"

Samson smiled.

Nike and Ares eyes were glued on the others, and they remained silent for a few minutes.

Nike began, "we were two of the best gladiators and we loved the game. The strategy, the practice, making it reality by transporting that ball across 100 yards and through the other team. We would script every pattern and every throw. We could sometimes overcome even the best athletes through teamwork and passion. And then..." he paused, "...the sweet thrill of victory.'

"It sounds like a glorious game," said Selene, whom had never seen the live version.

"Well, just like everything now, it evolved. It started out with protective pads and helmets, and rules to prevent injury, but the lords say the spectators are there for the violence. First they took away the pads, then the helmets. Then they allowed us to batter our way through the other team with our fists. Then they added obstacles to the field, first mud pits, walls, then barbed wire, and metal barriers. And then they added a spiked chain netting to the outside of the ball. Even carrying the prize caused injury. It has been that way for years now. Some call it 'war'ball, others bloodball." Nike explained.

"Bloodbaths sell," agreed Samson.

"And the dogs of war sleep when they are well fed," chanted Selene. Nike and Ares were startled by the statement.

"It's just something my father told me," she explained.

Ares took over, "And then came our last game. We knew we had to win to keep our positions. It may have been our greatest game, it was a masterpiece, but the other team was skilled as well. We executed sweeping, masterful plays that brought the ball up the field using a ladder of lateral passes. It truly was beautiful. We flung our bodies in front of theirs to halt their counter attacks. We were on the path to victory, but it was close. It was tied near the end of the match and we had the ball. I knew if we scored, it would be over. We tried several of the designed plays, but the other team figured them out. Both sides were dripping with blood, and we had lost several key players.'

Nike smiled, looked at Ares, and began, "That's when I saw the look in his eye. He knew what had to be done. Normally he played the 'general' position and dispersed the ball. I was lined up behind him to carry the ball after he passed it to me. A narrow gap opened straight ahead of him between the gladiators of the other team. I think we knew that along that path we both had a chance, but time was also running out.

"The action started, but Ares did not hand it off to me, and instead took it himself up the middle. He held it tight, so tight that it pierced his skin. He ran with a fury I'd never seen. Maybe he knew it would be his last run?

The players on the other side slashed and gauged at him, hitting his jaw and ribs. But Ares continued, and without a hint of hesitation. Their biggest player went for the ball and managed to tear it away, while dragging the spikes across Ares' stomach. But he didn't stop. Ares sent his shin out across the giant man's leg and brought him down with a crack. I think they might have broken each other's legs."

The story brought attention to Ares' swollen shin and the places where blood had soaked from his abdomen onto his jersey. Nike continued, "Ares picked up the ball again and ran. This time screaming with such a deep tone, that many might have mistaken him for a predatory animal. The other team's only chance was their fastest player—I think his name was Mercury—and he headed out after Ares. With twenty yards left Ares didn't dare look back. At about two yards from the goal line, Mercury caught him on his heal and tore off his shoe. This sent Ares tumbling across the line, but he had scored and then time ran out."

"And I think that bastard broke my ankle as well."

"We were victorious. Such a sweet taste. But Ares lay motionless in front of me on the ground just staring at the starry sky. I thought he might be dead, but I think he just realized something."

Ares took a deep breath and attempted to complete the story. "When Nike came to me, and I looked up at him from the red stained grass..." Ares suddenly slumped over onto the ground.

Nike lowered down to him. "He said he was done. We left the stadium and never looked back. We just left the bloodied ball outside the stadium."

Samson pulled out the bottle of whiskey he had collected near the flat rock, what now seemed like ages ago, and gave it to Nike. "Here, I don't need this anymore."

"Thank you." Ares eyes blinked and he looked up at the others. Nike lifted Ares' head up to the mouth of the whiskey bottle, and helped him to take several large swigs. Ares seemed to gasp in pleasure.

Nike also took a big swig of whiskey while looking down at his friend.

Selene went up to Ares and knelt at his side. He looked up at her. She felt his forehead gently. "He's burning up."

"Just like the fiery god, aye old friend," remarked Nike.

Ares smiled. "Just let me sleep, I'll be fine." And then he took another deep drink from the whiskey bottle. Selene handed him her canteen of water as well.

Nike looked to the others. "We walked for days, and I carried him as best as I could. And then we came to a large swamp. It was tough going. We actually made a flat raft and I pulled him along for some of the way. That swamp gave me strange vibes."

"Did you happen to come across an old hut in the middle of the swamp?" asked Samson.

"Hut? No, we saw no signs of another living soul. Why?"

"Eh, I just met someone in the swamp that seemed to possess some interesting qualities," answered Samson. Selene was looking at him in a peculiar way as he said this.

"I think I just hit the edge of the swamp," said Selene.

"We did get stalked by this strange alligator with one eye gauged out. Big guy. He followed us for a while, but then suddenly swung around as we came to the outer edge of the swamp.

"Then it was shortly after that we heard this gentleman whispering to the woods with his voice and guitar." Nike finished, looking at O.

O took the hint, and picked up the guitar and began to strum again. He did not sing this time and just played notes and melodies. Slowly, and one by one, the entire group began to close their eyes and fall asleep.

Samson watched the flames flicker through the closing cracks of his eyes. He was tired, but also clear about which way the journey should continue tomorrow. He had several thoughts that he knew he had to record and found a scrap of paper in his pocket. He used an old pencil to scribble the thoughts down, but kept them to himself. He wrapped the paper around several of the small translucent blue cubes in his pocket.

His mind returned to the music. The many thoughts from the discussions left him with words at the edge of his conscious and unconsciousness:

Celebrate

stagnation

or even a slight decay?

The water

does not stay

confined

in the reflective lake

forever.

It is evaporating,

freezing,

expanding against boundaries,

and flowing

into deep grooves.

The landscape

is not flat,

but ripples

under motion,

and feeds flames

with wood and oil.

Celebrate

the sun

warming our souls

from afar

and incinerating

broken orbits

and resurrecting bodies

as a focused incendiary.

Chapter 18: Lost in Sleep and Music

Light warmed and glowed through Samson's eyelids, so he opened them. The gleam of the morning came early and revealed the hidden details of the musician's home. The jagged edges of the broken aircraft fuselage were now clear. The intricate black woven fibers of its composite structure frayed from inside the edges of the wall, sandwiched between thin metal on both sides. Green tainted copper wires were left dangling from the edges in some places. Smooth rivets fastened the plastic facade of the interior to the walls, once giving an unblemished faux sense of luxury to the passengers.

Then Nike called out, "Oh Ares..."

Across the burnt out fire, Nike was holding the limp corpse of Ares in his arms. A few tears trailed down Nike's face. He whispered, "We had come so far, I thought we had won this battle as well. And what has this all been for? For all those victories on the field, you sacrificed everything, and now nothing is left. What a futile life we have lived."

The others also awoke to this scene and gathered around the two gladiators. "He died a warrior. He died beautifully, with the sounds of music," Selene said. Samson had not yet become accustomed to her poetic abilities.

Samson stepped forward and touched Nike on the shoulder, "Let us help you bury him."

They each carefully lifted a limb of Ares' body. "Where is that burial place you mentioned to us," Nike asked O.

O showed them to a clearing in the woods, where he had buried the bones of the passengers of the airliner. They found an undisturbed area near the edge of the clearing for Ares.

O only had one shovel, which he gave to Nike. The others used bowls and blades to cut and move the soil. With all of them working, it did not take them long to dig a shallow grave for Ares. Nike found some fragments of plastic from the plane that he fashioned into a tombstone for Ares. He used a knife to carve a message into the plastic. It read,

Here lies the general Ares,
A god among men.
Rest in peace
my friend.

The group stood in silence around the grave for some time, and then Nike asked, "So, where are we going?"

Samson and Selene looked at each other. Samson responded, "Well, I have not had any need to go anywhere in a long time, but I think she does. There is an island near the coast, probably not far from here, where they seem to be trying to build something new."

Nike ears perked up, "well that does sound interesting. How do you know where it is or that we'll be there when we find it?"

"There was a picture of a red and white striped lighthouse in a flyer."

Selene began digging through her pockets and pulled out the worn brochure with the beautiful picture of the cottages and the lighthouse. "Here, this is it. Of course this is what it looked like before the Fall."

Nike gently took the brochure and examined it. "This does look enticing. Do you think they are still there? Do you think they have succeeded? I may have heard of legends of some place like this. Ares..." He looked around as if to find a leaving individual, but his eyes fell to the mound of dirt. "Ares and I heard of a place like this. You hear interesting things in the locker rooms of a blood ball match. I never thought something like this really existed. I never thought it was possible. There was never any real evidence."

"One of our friends, she, well, she actually was also born there. So it does exist, at least when she was growing up there. I guess that was no more than five years ago?" said Selene.

"Where is she?" said O.

Nike could see something in how Selene's body drooped when she said it. He knew and acknowledged it, "She's with Ares ain't she?"

Selene nodded.

"She and Ares might have been formed from the same hard shell. They are probably telling stories over a good drink now," said Samson. "But her other half is also missing."

"Other half?" asked Nike.

"Yes, this fiery lad named Elio. They were also building something. I am not sure if it would have reached the same heights, but it fell, and I might be to blame," acknowledged Samson.

"Why?" asked Nike.

"He isn't," corrected Selene. "Let the past be the past. We are here now. Let's follow a path to somewhere with more light."

"So this is to the east?" asked O.

"Yes"

"You know there are miles of marsh between the mainland and the coastal islands? You should find a solid road and follow it," pointed out O.

Samson nodded, "I've also been this way before, but never to this specific island. You're right."

Selene looked a little disgusted with having to follow a road. Samson responded, "It is the only option. I also am not one to follow the concrete, nor the asphalt, but we have no business crossing the marsh on foot."

"Could find a boat," remarked Nike.

"I've never seen any around here," added O.

"You don't sound like you're comin'?" asked Nike.

"Yeah, I'm too old for new places. I belong with the lost souls. Maybe I'll write a song about you all and this mythical lighthouse."

"Naw, we need your music on the road," said Nike.

"Maybe I'll be a beacon for the other travelers destined to follow your path. If it is true, there will be more. I am sure they could all benefit from a welcoming water hole and a subpar song," O thought out loud.

"You have been a beacon your entire life. You are an opening in the fabric to universal beauty. But, I understand. My bones too grow rooted to this ground," Samson said and then looked at Selene, "and yet my path has not yet ended...and neither has yours. Even if you don't move in this physical world, you are moving and changing in the realm that matters."

Selene produced a barely noticeable smile.

They all walked back to the fuselage. Still midday, the top of the painted metal gleamed.

"I think we should leave now," said Nike.

Samson agreed, because he knew how fast roots grew from soles and souls into the dark ground. He nodded in agreement, as did Selene.

They all began packing up their belongings into their packs. Samson came across the lighter/solar powered survival device he had found at the store where he had met Selene. It had a sound recording mechanism built into it. He sat his pack down and brought it toward O. O turned toward him.

"Do you still record?" Samson asked. He opened a compartment in the back of the recording device and out tumbled two crystal recording cubes. These were the same type of cubes Samson had wrapped in the paper and dreamed of in the treasure chest. He held them up in front of the sun. "You can record a lot of songs on one of these."

"I haven't, in years."

"These cubes keep information safe for centuries," Samson pointed out. "Maybe they will be discovered again?"

"I thought that there was no one left to listen. Maybe I thought wrong?"

Samson gripped O's hands, and stared at his eyes, "There is, there always will be. This might not have the best sound quality, but Robert Johnson didn't record with the best quality either…and thank you. For this, now and before. I used to write. Mostly gibberish, but I stopped. Maybe I shouldn't have."

O looked as Samson and without a nod or a word, paused and showed a deep agreement. After an iron moment, he said, "we are a diminishing breed. We are the past, but we can still help shape the future. I did forget that, but I won't ever again."

Samson returned to packing. Soon everyone had their pack on, except Nike, who was finishing one he had been making from parts he found in the fuselage carcass. He had used seatbelts for the shoulder straps, and cut the seat fabric to use as cushioning and the actual bag itself. The back of his pack displayed the emblem of the airline, a red triangular arrowhead shape.

They all took some time to thank O and say goodbye. Nike seemed to take the longest.

"So, do you have any idea where a road is?" Asked Samson to O. Selene also pulled out the brochure of the lighthouse island. A simple map was printed on its back. Someone had also drawn in additional details, such as natural landmarks. The marshes had been etched on as reeds and labeled.

O held the map and examined it. He then pointed to a location on the far left edge, and far from the island. "I believe we are about right here, just north of this main highway that heads almost directly out to the coast. So I'd just head south until you hit that road and then follow it east. Experienced folks like you shouldn't have too many problems. Now get along."

"We'll tell tales about you," said Selene.

"I'll tell visitors about you as well, but mine will sound better," he said smirking. "If it doesn't work out, you are all welcome back here."

"I am sure you will have more visitors, especially if this place does exist," said Nike.

Nike then tightened the seatbelt straps of his crafted pack. Samson and Selene were also all ready to depart. They turned and began heading toward a gap in the forest.

"Hold on, I have one more song before you go," insisted O.

O picked up his old guitar. He tilted it to empty some leaves and debris that had gathered inside the hollow body. He also tuned each string by gently plucking each tendon and twisting the connecting knobs at the end of the instruments neck.

He then began to strum. The notes blended together not only with the other notes emitting from the mouth of the acoustic guitar, but with the singing of the birds and the rustling of the leaves in the wind. He followed the fast clicks of a woodpecker, which followed with a pause every four taps. The wood trees creaked at longer wavelengths that still harmonized with the music.

Then O began to sing. The lyrics and music did not follow the usually cycle of refrains separated by a repeated chorus. It followed a different natural progressive structure, like the Australian aboriginals would use song to mark their paths across a continent and life. His words were harmonious and clear,

"The light rotates
from a cindering flame
reflecting off a disk
as round as the moon,
across the world,
and into the cracks
of every ruin,
and the patterns
in every stone wall,
and every tree bark
wrinkle,
every leathered face,
casting shadows
behind mountains
marking the location
of hull cracking rocks,
that gather the souls
of lost sailors
who don't know
that they were searchin'
for a mythical island
containin' treasures
written only in the stars."

Chapter 19: Definitions

As the three walked, a cool wind grew and began to surge against their backs, like a snow-melt river pushing floating logs toward the sea. Rather than the result of a melting summer, however, this air was bringing winter.

They each were trees, severed from birth, their bodies slowly decaying as they rushed toward an open horizon. Samson had been floating the longest, and his wood was rotting faster and faster, and soaking in more and more water. He feared that at some point he would no longer float, and just sink and become lodged on the floor of the widening river. Nike was not as old, but his body had been hacked by axes and lumberjack saws that had never completed their cuts. His bark had been breached long ago, which allowed the parasites to enter and consume him.

Samson looked ahead and the live oaks clasped their fingers together into a canopy of leaves and Spanish moss. The ground was a mix of soil and sand. Periodically they came upon patches of palmetto shrubs, which resembled the tops of palm trees on the ground. The jagged leaves of the palmettos left a sandy maze of paths between them. Samson knew these were great areas for rodents and their predators.

Selene had walked ahead and was almost out of Samson's sight when she suddenly stopped. The forest filled with the distinctive alarm buzz of a rapidly shaking container of loose parts. Samson knew what it was without seeing it. He drew the still shiny knife that Selene had given him.

Samson and Nike soon caught up to Selene and paused behind her, examining the coiled snake with brown diamond patterns on the path ahead. Its skin created a tapestry that would rival the rugs of any Persian palace. Samson identified the serpent immediately as an Eastern Diamondback Rattlesnake—once considered the most dangerous of snakes in this region.

Nike raised his fist and the same knife he had caught Samson by surprise with. He began to creep closer toward the snake. The snake rattled his tail with increasing rigor, but Nike ignored its warning. It slowly drew its head back into its coil as if cocking the hammer of a deadly firearm.

"Hold it," Samson said firmly, but calmly, so as not to disturb the snake. Samson put his hand gently on Nike's raised arm and forced it down, and then directed him backwards. The snake's rattling lowered by several decibels, and was less frantic.

Once they were again safe distance from the snake, Samson only said, "This is his home more than ours. We can go around."

Selene found an opening to the left that lead to a meandering path through the palmetto brush. As Samson followed, he thought about how these trails through the palmetto brush often followed an indirect path that resembled the detail of Brownian motion. The brush consisted of saw palmetto as well, and one had to be weary of the jagged edges of the braches. That saw tooth patterned edge was an important detail of the palmetto brush structure. It protected not only the plant, but larger animals from entering the brush. Therefore the brush made an advantageous home for small animals and rodents. That rattlesnake was also another essential detail in the pattern. It filled a critical role in the hierarchy of the foodchain. Without it, the rodents would overpopulate, and maybe eventually take down the palmetto brush ecosystem and the habitat itself.

There were so many parts in the ecosystem—so many details—like a fractal geometry of an intricate layer of geometries. So where did humans fit into this hierarchal fractal of a world? Samson had also thought about this in detail during his journeys alone through the fallen landscape. He had concluded that we were merely a detail. Nonetheless, every detail is just as essential as every other detail. Without humans, this would not be the same earth. Without saw palmettos, this would not be the same earth. Without rattlesnakes, this would not be the same earth. Without entangling vines, this would not be the same earth. Each and every detail provided the defining boundary for each and every other detail.

Soon they left the palmetto brush and were walking on a flat and sandy pine grove.

Nike joined Samson at his side, and took the opportunity to express some concerns. Selene was far ahead of them and barely in sight between the gaps in the trees. "Ya think they will let a flagrant like me into this place?"

"Of course they would. I doubt they'd let me in if they don't let you in," Samson said, trying to be convincing. Why did he suddenly feel like he had to keep this band together?

"Naw, you've got a rustic nobility about you. While I'm just a washed up mercenary."

Samson thought a moment, and realized the similarity of this concern to their experience in the palmetto brush. "Just as that snake belongs, so do you. Everything has a role and we all are pieces in this vast puzzle."

"Well, that island is not my home...and most folks never want rattlesnakes in their home," Ares pointed out with sincere concern.

Samson shrugged, "Hopefully they won't judge rattlesnakes by their fangs and their previous meals...or maybe we'll just drop off the kid there." Nike smiled at the joke and replied,

"...maybe she's dropping us off."

Samson laughed, and said, "I am not sure if what's left of the world is ready for her."

Selene must have heard them talking and circled around and came up behind them suddenly. Samson did not think she heard much though.

"What are you old birds squawking about?" Selene asked with a smile. Samson had not seen her smile much since he met her. Her smile was infectious and everyone now seemed to be in a good mood, despite all the witnessed darkness.

"Well, if it is as utopian as we've heard, I'm sure they'll meet us with open arms," remarked Samson.

Nike responded, "I'm not so sure. I've heard that they were once open, but are now guarded due to some unsavory folks trying to take advantage of the situation. I heard something about there being exiles, but if you are noble and true, that you'll get in. Someone said something about trials or questions they use to judge you."

"Just like standing at the pearly gates and trying to convince ole' Saint Peter," interjected Samson.

Looking at Samson and then at Selene, Nike said "Well, whatever we find, I think we will be in your debt. They might let us in with you at our side."

Following that remark, Selene drew out her atlatl and slung a spear quickly into the distance. Samson's reflexes caused him to draw his knife. He squinted in the direction of the spear. Barely in sight, an animal squawked, scurried for a moment, and fell. When Samson looked to Selene, she was already halfway to the animal.

Nike and Samson followed quickly. They came upon Selene standing over a large wild turkey on the ground with the spear stuck into its breast. Samson looked to Nike and nodded. Nike put his hand on Samson's arm, as if to brace himself. His other hand drew out to Selene. Selene picked up the turkey and handed it by its legs to Nike.

"We can cook it later tonight," said Samson. Nike cleaned it quickly, except for the feathers, and slung it over his shoulder. They then continued on their way.

"We should be reachin' that road soon. Let's keep on our toes," said Selene, putting her weapon back in its holster.

They walked for a little ways. Selene did not rush ahead as before. After an hour or so of silence, she asked, "so...what's everyone's real names?"

"I haven't gone by my real name in so long," Nike said contemplatively.

Samson looked at them and then to the path ahead, "How do you know Samson's not my real name?"

Selene gave him a grimacing look in return.

"Listen, that snake we crossed back there, it was an Eastern Diamondback Rattlesnake, but that is just a label. Does the name define the creature? It is much more than just that label or name. We are made of infinite amounts of detail, and are not easily described. I'm happy with Samson...you happy with Nike...you happy with Selene? If so, let's leave it at that. After all, that's who we are to each other."

Selene seemed to agree, but suddenly had the look he had seen when they left her town, and she had stopped by the smoldering house.

"My parents had given me a name, but they were also content to stay in that town. Because they were so content, that was the name they gave me. They are still in that town, with nothing else now. But since you know me as something else, I suppose we should continue as we are."

Nike said, "Well, however you acquired Selene, it's a good one. You see, in our, I mean my past business, you have limited education, except when it comes to sports figures of the previous ages, including gladiators and mythology..."

"Hence Nike and Ares..."

"Yeah, and many others. Including women warriors...One of the biggest draws in that stadium...there was one, so beautiful that they named her after the moon, after Selene, goddess of the moon."

"It does seem to suit her," Samson agreed. Even more than that, she was a light in these dark times. Perhaps her light was reflected from somewhere else, that he did not know, but it was still bright. She was a light in this age of night.

Selene did not say anything else in response. How does one fill the shoes of a goddess?

The three walked on until the sun grew dim. In the coming darkness they could see the pale surface of a bleached road ahead. The sight of the road still ignited a sense of alarm within Samson. What was he doing? Had he gone mad? Actually planning to follow a road? Well, based on his company things had definitely changed considerably over the past few weeks.

"Let's stop here but drawback from the road a bit," suggested Samson. The others agreed.

They emptied their packs and started a fire to cook the turkey. Nike pulled all of the feathers and prepared the bird on a spit suspended above the flames. As it cooked, the smell of cooking turkey filled the camp area and ignited their appetites. After they were certain it was fully cooked, they divided it up as best as they could. Nike asked Selene which parts she wanted first, because she had killed it.

Soon they all had a piece and began to eat. Selene ate from a large leg. It was somewhat humorous because it made her appear almost primitive. Perhaps it was because Samson could recall medieval reenactment festivals, at which people then thought barbarians walked around eating huge turkey legs.

"So tomorrow, we take to the road," remarked Nike between bites.

"Yes, and we should be all the more careful. A road is where we lost the others, and Rhodus, who probably travelled this same road when leaving the island," replied Selene.

"Well, I think this road is a little different than the other. Most of it is on land rising from the marsh on both sides. That will make it more difficult for concealment," said Samson, thinking out loud.

"Foes can't hide, but we won't be able to either," said Selene.

"At least we'll be able see what's coming," remarked Nike.

"...and what's going," thought Samson. He wondered if others were still making their way to this *mythical* island. Or would there be others already leaving because they did not find what they wanted? Encountering either might be useful.

"Tomorrow is a big day, we should get some sleep," suggested Selene. The tryptophan in the turkey started to make Samson tired. Selene and Nike also hunched and drooped to the ground.

The nights were growing colder. Samson unrolled his patchwork sleeping bag and climbed in. He watched the smoke from the fire slowly diminish as the flames died out. He almost wondered if he could still recall his given name. For all those years he spoke to very few, and those who did never referred to him by name. And now he had this name given to him by an inquiring young leader. Samson's eyes closed.

In the dark,
without the moon,
the paths
can only be discerned
from the paved road,
by touch.
But on the old maps
the lines marking them
were thicker
and often patterned,
labeled;
sometimes
with merely a number.

Chapter 20: The Gate

The three all rose early the next day. They merged onto the road with little excitement. Samson walked to the center of the road, where a dashed yellow line was still visible on the cracked asphalt. The air was cold. The wind felt cooler on the road, perhaps because it blew unobstructed. The oscillating ocean breeze, changing directions from night to day, now pressed inward to the land. Walls of trees still lined each side of the road, acting as a funnel for the wind from the unseen marshes and beaches ahead. They walked against the wind.

Selene found that the wind was slower near the tree line and followed it along-side the road when she could. Samson, although he hated the road, preferred the center, where one could see farther around the bends ahead. Nike went back and forth between the two—unsure of either. Sometimes a ditch filled with water runoff from the road pushed Selene to either leave the road or to enter into the woods.

The trees suddenly disappeared. After walking for an hour, they had reached the marshes. Here, the flow of the sea was trapped by barrier islands. Samson stopped again. The air smelled of salt. The reeds of the marsh vibrated with the now dispersed wind. Far in the distance, the rumble of the ocean and its ever churning thermodynamic engine could be heard.

The vast ocean ahead remained cool, while the land heated in the day. The strength of the ocean sent its winds deep into the land, in an attempt to cool it.

This marsh was the source of new life. Small fish learned to escape, and others learned to hunt. The larger fish would rarely explore this far away from the deep, and so life had created its own structure that differed from the swallowing deep blue sea. This was the estuary.

The shallow water also warmed faster in the sunlight. The dark mud below the water absorbed the heat and stored it for the night. These waters acted as an incubator for eggs, and the future. The violent but renewing cycle of life was here, yet on a smaller scale, resulting in an illusion of tranquility.

Now the three could see far out into the distances around them. A few islands rose from the marsh where oaks and palm trees had taken root. The deeper parts of the marsh also contained channels, large enough for boats, entangling like a labyrinth in the marsh. Man had clearly created this straight road through the marsh, because it did not follow any of the patterns. In the deep channels were still the heavily decayed maritime markers for boats. Their wood columns thinned at the water line. Oysters and barnacles collected on the wood there, and slowly ate away at it. A few of the markers had already fallen and left only sharp stumps peaking above the water. Others appeared to be held up only by the shells.

Samson thought about the first people who crossed these marshes. They probably would have used boats to cross them, not all too different from Karon's raft that he and Selene had crossed the long lake upon. This body of water was different. They were finally leaving the realm that they had entered upon over the lake, and were now crossing into something else.

Soon the three were all forced by the marsh to walk on the cracked road, or on the narrow sliver of grass on each side. Old power lines also followed the road, but most of them had lay limp or snapped on the ground. Samson mistook them a few times for a black snake out of the corner of his eye. Clearly, they were now lifeless.

They could see a small structure far ahead of them on the left side of the road. As they came closer, the painted words, "Pilgrims Welcome," could be made out on a ragged sign above the porch.

"We must be on the right path," remarked Nike. Selene took out her knife and crept into the building. Samson followed her and Nike inside. At one time this confined space was fully occupied.

Near the front windows leaned signs marking the prices for items, mostly items that travelers would be in need of after a long journey. One read 'Water,' with a price marked in a currency similar to the one used in the town Nike came from. The next looked to be 'Peanuts,' and another had been marked just with 'Preserved Meat.' The last said 'Sacred Oil.' That caught Selene's eye.

"What would you do with sacred oil?" she asked.

Nike started, "hmmm, well some people might burn it, releasing its aroma. Depends on what it was I suppose. Some might put it on their skin..." which caused Samson to think of the oiled women once again from Nike's town. He did not think of them as sacred, but perhaps they were. The flesh is sacred, in that it is a vessel for our souls.

"...others might consume a little..." then Nike smirked, "...but I've seen most just leave it on a shelf, never to be used."

Behind a counter Selene pulled out some wrinkled papers. The paper had been wet at some time and were discolored and lines of mold had grown on them. Nonetheless, Samson immediately recognized them. They were copies of the same brochure showing the lighthouse and cottages that he had found in his stash of materials near the flat rock—the same brochure he had burned in the fire, the same one Selene had brought with her, along with the article on entanglement.

Nike said, "Well I'll be damned. Guess this is definitely the right way."

"Yes, but it doesn't look like any pilgrims have passed through in a while. Perhaps the island has already drifted into legend? Like Atlantis?" added Selene. The same grim thought had also crossed his mind. What if this place no longer existed? Why had it sunk beneath the fate of this age? Had they seen a fate similar to the crescents, or was it something even more tragic?

"It may be that this place's time has passed, or it may be nothing," agreed Samson.

In the back of the single room shack lay the metal frame and spring of a small bed. The bedding fabric was still there, but rotting away. It had been a long time since someone had slept here.

"Well, let's keep moving," suggested Samson. They all exited the shack through an open doorway, with rusted hinges still intact from where a door once was.

The three spilled out onto the bleached road once again. It appeared whiter and more decayed than the roads farther inland. Maybe the salty air was to blame? Or perhaps lower the grains of sand penetrating into the cracks and prying them open? Or perhaps the lack of shade allowed the sun to scorch the road from sunrise to sunset?

Occasionally they would see an animal scurry across the road. Lizards sunbathing themselves would wait until the travelers were a few feet away until they would disappear into the foliage.

They soon came across an ancient looking gopher tortoise crossing the road. The tortoise was full grown and larger than a human head. He did not scurry. He did not run. He did not seem concerned, until one of them tried to pick him up.

"Before the Fall, when some people were so tangled up in technology that they had lost their connection to nature, we would stop and help them across," Samson recalled, and then winced, from the painful memory. He remembered the pop of one unfortunate turtle beneath the tire of a truck, driven by someone either disconnected or connected to the wrong outlet. "It was not uncommon to come across crushed shells on the roads just like this, but this one doesn't have to worry. He might be older than I, and be wondering, 'what happened to all of the metallic beasts that followed these hard paths?' He probably prefers this things this way."

"He is a wise one," Selene agreed, as she bent down closer to the wrinkled face. The tortoise opened his sharp beaked mouth and let out a hissing gasp.

"He reminds me of you," she added, looking up at Samson.

"Alright you tree huggers," Nike exclaimed. Samson wondered how that term had survived.

They each passed the tortoise and continued down the road. The marsh changed little, but did cross several wider areas, that prior to the road were isolated islands.

Far ahead, a larger land crossing slowly came into view. It appeared to be another road crossing the one they were on. In the middle of the crossroads, another small structure came into view. As they came closer, two figures emerged from it.

"Well, we knew we'd meet someone at some point," remarked Nike.

The three were still far away, and so they could not make out many details. One figure held something up to his eyes. Perhaps binoculars? If so, they held the advantage and already knew more about Samson, Selene and Nike.

"Just take it easy," Samson said. "Most likely they are friendly." His hand yearned for the handle of his sheathed knife.

Nike began to draw out the same knife he had held to Samson's throat just a few days ago.

Selene motioned to Nike to leave it, "we won't need them, just yet."

They walked steadily and carefully toward the crossroads.

"Ain't the crossroads where one meets the devil?" asked Nike. "Told y'all, we'd hear all kinds of yarns in the backrooms of the stadium. Even heard that a certain wandering minstrel inked a deal with the red horned fellow. Maybe this is where it all went down? Maybe our pal O signed it all away here?" Nike said with a light chuckle. "Sorry, I always tell jokes before a battle."

"Let's stay positive," corrected Selene.

The details of the figures came into focus. They both held long metal objects, most likely rifles.

"Still think they are peaceful?" asked Nike.

"Even utopia needs protecting," Samson pointed out.

"Is it utopia then?" pondered Selene.

They said nothing else during the remaining half mile to the shack. As they came closer they could see that this was some sort of gateway, and that the two figures were guards. The guards looked like they had been living at this remote location for weeks. They wore patched together military fatigues. Their clothing was stained reddish brown from blood in several locations, either from hunted animals, or other travelers. They both had scraggly un-kept beards. One's beard was not as full as the other, and had lighter brown hair.

The guard with the deep dark forest of a beard stepped forward, holding his firearm barrel pointed loosely at the three. His finger hovered on the trigger. He said in a raspy voice, the kind you get from being sick and dehydrated, "Y'all best head back from where you came. There ain't nothin' out there no more."

"We just wanted to get to the ocean. We hear it's this way," Samson said smirking. Selene did not appear to find amusement in Samson's joking.

"There's plenty of other ways to ocean," the scraggly bearded one said.

Selene asked in a frank voice, "Is the lighthouse still standing?"

"We've got bad news for you little one, it fell long ago. There was a battle, a gruesome one."

"We'd like to see for ourselves," said Nike.

"You want to join us? You willing to do what's necessary to keep the peace?" suggested the dark bearded one. He then noticed a tattoo on Nike's arm of an eagle carrying a spiked ball.

"You're one of those war ball athletes, ain't cha? Why you leaving the big city and the game?"

"Retirement," replied Nike.

"We could probably use someone like you, but there's a vetting process. You and the girl can wait here and we'll send someone over to take you there," the guard replied.

The other guard with less beard seemed to disagree. "I don't think they've got what it takes. Let's just dispose of these two and take the girl. We could have some fun with her."

The dark bearded one gave him a look in agreement, but also in staking his claim on the spoils.

Samson didn't like where this was going.

Selene's gaze was fierce, "we all go. Step aside." She drew and knocked a spear in her atlatl with the blink of an eye.

Samson made a suggestion, "perhaps we can make a payment?" He searched through the pockets and held out the six remaining crescent cut coins.

The sparsely bearded one give a dark chuckle. "Those bits of metal mean nothing here. I've got more valuable metal in this beauty here. Want to trade?" The guard held up the rifle and peered down the barrel toward Samson.

Samson tapped the hilt of his knife with his hand.

The full bearded guard remarked, "you ain't that fast. Ain't no one that fast, even someone who's seen as many moons as..."

A swift shadow then flew from a palmetto shrub growing near the edge of the marsh. It negated the threat of the two guards in what seemed like one swift motion. When he stopped, Samson and Selene immediately recognized him.

Elio, soaking wet from the marsh, stood before them.

"I've been listening to them squabble for weeks. It's a shame it ended this way."

"Elio!" exclaimed Selene. She showed a genuine smile.

"What the hell you doing out here?" asked Samson.

"I've been waiting in a thicket on that island out there. I kind of figured that you all might eventually head this way, and if not, this seemed like a noble place to start."

"Start what?" inquired Nike.

"A final stand...let's tie these two up. They're just unconscious. We can stay here tonight without worry. They rarely checked on these guys. They just would send a telegraph code in every day or so."

The sea breeze had reached its peak and now seemed slow as the day's end came into sight. They found several pieces of cord that the guards appeared to have for tying up prisoners, and used it to tie up the guards.

Samson took a moment to look across the marsh. In the distance it seemed to widen and deepen, as it opened up to the sea. A few scarce words came to his mind.

> On the scale
> of organisms,
> the cycle began
> and ended.

On the scale
of atoms
the vibrations
blurred.
On the scale
of the stars
both
were smooth.

Chapter 21: All Prophets

The four built a small fire in a pit that the guards had used. They were eating what turkey remained and taking the time to reacquaint themselves. The stars exposed themselves above.

"So what's your story, what is it, Nike?" Elio asked, once they had all settled down.

"Well, you might have guessed that I'm an ex-baller, gladiator, or whatever you want to call us. Now I'm just looking for a better life." Nike replied.

"We all are, but now that's not enough, you must make one for yourself," argued Elio.

"Well, I see someone hasn't lost much fire," proclaimed Samson. Elio drew a knife in response and slung it toward Samson. The blade lodged in the stump Samson was sitting on. But Samson was amazed. This man had been completely broken. Had lost everything, and not in one blow. First it was the village he had poured his energy into to create. Then, after that was taken away, his love was taken away. All that he had left...gone.

Looking down, Samson wiggled the knife free and admired it. He replied, "You know, I've been there. I've fallen so far. But I lost the very framework of who I was as well..."

"Who says I haven't," said Elio. Tears were flowing down from his eyes to his mouth. Selene moved next to him, and tried to comfort him.

Nike commented, "We're a stable bunch aren't we? You aren't the one from this lighthouse island, are you?"

Selene corrected him, "No, she was his lighthouse."

"Oh," said Nike.

Elio gasped, and seemed to regain his composure, and maybe his sanity. "I've seen it, Rho's island. It's real. It's all true."

"Is it standing, the lighthouse?" asked Selene.

"It is, and it still shines a light across the harbor at night. Actually we can probably see it from here," Elio said, pointing east toward the ocean.

Everyone stood up, except Elio, and gazed down the road toward the ocean. The light pulsed brightly. They all let its energy enter them.

While still standing, Selene asked Elio, who was still sitting, "Was there a war?"

"I would say that the war has really not yet begun. These guards...the stories they tell people," Elio said shaking his head.

"What are they guarding then? Aren't they on our side?"

"No, they are the one's planning to attack the island. It is surrounded. I am not sure who they are, but they have firepower. It appears that the islanders also blew the bridges onto the island as a way to protect themselves. I can tell though, these guys and their friends are planning to move soon. They have boats."

"We need to do something," said Selene.

"Hold on now, I didn't sign up on some crusade," said Nike, shaking his head. He looked back from the still pulsing lighthouse to Elio, who was gazing deep into the fire.

Selene stepped back between them and looked at Nike, "you've been a fighter, a warrior, your entire life. Except you were always fighting for nothing, now you have something."

"Well, I was always fighting for my life, and a bit of glory. But never something like this. When the game was over, the war ended. If we start this, an ending might not be so simple. And what about you?" he asked, looking squarely at Samson.

Samson turned from the lighthouse in the distance and sat next to Elio. They both gazed deeply into the fire.

He began to answer, "I once had a raging fire within me. I would take every path, turn every stone, in my search."

"What were you searching for?" asked Elio.

"My family, at least at first. But then something else guided me. I can't explain what it was. Maybe instinct? To others it probably seemed like madness. But perhaps I was just a particle in a river—that once fought the current—but then let it take me. Where the current is taking us, I do not know." At that moment the wind shifted and began to blow from the land to the sea. The land had cooled to a temperature lower than the ocean, and now in the night it cooled the ocean in return for the ocean cooling it during the heat of day. The breeze pushed Samson toward the coast and the island. His white curly hair flowed like the cresting waves on a stormy sea. He continued, "Now, I feel like this may be a new beginning, as the river meets the ocean, so to speak."

Elio's eyes remained glued on Samson but his body shifted when the wind changed. Somehow Elio and Samson were floating on the same river, but at different points. Elio had taken faster currents over many miles, while Samson had at times swirled in the eddies behind the rocks. Samson was never stationary, but gathering energy for the final trek. Now, somehow they were floating almost next to each other. Elio was a young branch, still with some green leaves, and dense with sap, while Samson was a water-logged branch who's bark had been worn away long ago. Now the surfaces of the old log were smooth and bleached in the sun, like driftwood. Samson knew that they would embark onto the ocean together, or at least in each other's sight. They were synchronized.

"But the water does not end in the ocean, it continues the cycle, to find the river again one day," said Selene.

Samson nodded, as did Elio.

Nike returned to the fire next to them. "So what's our plan? How could we make an impact?"

The fire reflected in Elio's eyes. "I've given that some thought. I know where their armory is. It's guarded, but we could get in. Maybe we could release all that chemical energy in the weapons there? They've been manufacturing some of their own gunpowder, but their process is messy. I'm pretty sure that place would go up easily with one well-placed spark."

"Ok. Have you been to the island?" asked Nike.

"No, but I've seen it from a distance," replied Elio.

"Is it utopia?"

"What's utopia? How would you paint it? It may or may not be it, but it is alive. The island actually reminds me...of our village. The one Rho and I helped organize. Perhaps some of her youth on the island rubbed off on the village...but those days are gone."

"Where did your village come from?" asked Samson,

"What do you mean?" Elio replied, although he was seeing what Samson was asking.

"Why were there no others of my age?" asked Samson.

"Well, we had all lived in a larger city, far from here. A large number of people from the age before the Fall had gathered there. We lived comfortably. The city was clean and safe. They had even managed to refit several solar power stations that gave us electricity. I was born, just before the Fall, but do not remember it. Being raised in that city, I always thought that the time before the Fall would be a lot like it." Elio paused and looked at Samson.

Samson received the cue, "It sounds like it was and it wasn't. Once you've witnessed a change as rapid as the Fall, you cannot return to what you were before. In my wanderings I may have visited your city. I remember a place somewhere meeting your description, but I felt trapped and left."

"Just like you did in our village." Elio remarked.

"Did your parents survive?" asked Selene.

Elio shook his head from side to side and then began again, "They were also lost in the Fall. I have very little memory of them. Some friends of our family found me and raised me. I have to admit, it was then a nourishing childhood.

"They were a stagnant people, those who raised me, and almost the entire city. They were not caught in eddies, they were not even connected to the flowing river, but rather were isolated pools. Some were waiting to dry up. The wise ones were more like tidal pools, waiting for the ocean to come rescue them. But I realized that it might never arrive."

"But you could always dig them canals, to reconnect them. You had to try?" remarked Selene.

Elio tried to explain, "Have you ever tried to dig paths in the dirt to direct water? It is hard, and the water will always follow the direction of gravity. It also is stronger than the soil, eroding it and eventually creating its own path. Don't hear me wrong, they were strong. They had to be, to survive and to live on. They were rocks, but the kind that do not roll.

That is why I've always had respect for you Samson, even in my snickering."

Samson touched Elios shoulder and said "They might have been stronger than I. I just fell into a different way."

Elio continued, "They did have children after the Fall. Maybe that was their final gift to the world? Those children brought with them an untainted perspective, but some of the original traits of their parents seeped in, and as they grew toward adulthood, they sought to find their own way, as they all do. For some reason they began to look up to me. Even though I was from before the Fall, I didn't remember it, and was aligned more with the next generation. They wanted out. They wanted to find the flowing water. I honestly wasn't so sure yet.

"About this time I met Rho. We had a connection I had never felt before. She told stories about the island and the place she came from, but she did not want to return. She also had a desire to create something new. She had traveled all that distance nearly on her own. She had learned the skills of survival, either on her own, or on the island, and she brought them to us.

So we, the youth of the city, started to meet and plan. It took a long time for us to obtain the confidence to leave. It took even longer for us to gain the required knowledge and skills to survive. You see, the elders, those from the previous age, still were partially stuck in that time. They still depended on some of those methods and some of those ideas. We had campouts, disguised as youth retreats, where we worked on the skills they never taught us." Samson chuckled to himself, as this reminded him of his time in the youth scout program. It sounded similar, but with different motives. The elder people of the city would have suspected nothing.

Elio took a deep breath. The others could tell that he was nearing the end his story. He went on, "Then one night, I remember it clearly, we packed our things. Some of us already had children, so we brought them, and in the middle of the night, no really the early morning, we left. It was a full moon that night, and as we left, it followed us. That is when it began to inspire me and it gave me the idea to share its inspiration with the others.

At first we used electric vehicles available in the city. After a several hundred miles, they stopped. They did allow us to cross the steep mountains of the west. Then we walked. We knew to fully separate that we would have to journey far away, and to leave little trace, which is difficult with that many people. Unfortunately we did lose some along the way. Eventually, we came upon a deserted town. We occupied it and that is where you found us."

A nearly full moon now began to rise above the tree line. Samson couldn't help but to think of the eclipse and when he had first seen Elio speaking to the villagers that night in the woods. He reached in his pocket and drew out the six remaining crescent coins and gave them to Elio. Elio held up one coin to cover the moon above, except where the off center circle had been cut, allowing pale light through.

"So what gave you that idea for the eclipse?" asked Samson.

"I had found an old book about stargazing and it contained a detailed list of future celestial events. I wanted so much for the world to change. I made myself believe that the eclipse would bring the change, or maybe the night sky led me to believe."

"I failed to appreciate what you did before, but I see it more now," admitted Samson.

Elio continued, "Even if the eclipse was not truly bringing change, we are all a piece of the same universe, just as the moon, so by it merely existing and following its act, isn't it already leading us? I just decided to follow it." He said looking around the fire first at Nike, then Samson and then Selene, who was still looking at the lighthouse, but whose pale complexion now glowed in the night. She was the force causing the tides to push back into the mouth of the river, and then releasing it and draining it out to the sea.

"What happened to your parents?" Elio asked Selene.

Samson knew that the question would again come, and hoped that she was now ready to answer it. Travelling as they had seemed to have a healing power, which maybe was why he had done it for all these years.

Selene did not answer immediately. Nike touched her shoulder and said, "You do not need to answer if you don't want to."

"No, it's time...we were pretty much alone in that town. That was where Samson found me. I am not sure what happened to the rest of those that survived the Fall. Maybe they just left for a bigger city?

We had plenty of left over remnants in the town, but my mother and father were resourceful and lived off the surrounding land. They taught me all they knew. They were very content and maybe protective. They did not want to leave, especially not before I was older, but I am not sure when that would have been.

We would meet people on rare occasions. Some would arrive proclaiming the promise of their new civilizations and asking us to join them. We would decline every time. Some came for the resources, and mostly did not bother us. Maybe they didn't always even know that we were there. One night..." she paused and turned from the lighthouse and sat down.

"That cold night, several travelers must have seen our fire and came to our house. At other times we had hosted visitors peacefully, but my parents, they saw something they did not like in them. Maybe they were consuming alcohol or another mind altering material. Maybe they could tell that their minds were not at ease.

They had trained me to leave and hide in such a situation, so I did. I am not sure what happened after that, but I heard fighting and in the morning the house was caught on fire. I was too scared to get close. The people soon left, but the house was burnt to the ground.

I lived on my own for some time in another house, but I made sure to stay in the shadows. I am not sure why we revealed ourselves to each other." Selene finished, looking toward Samson.

Everyone was now silent. The bonds between them strengthened. Bonded not just with the knowledge of each tale, but of the tales themselves. The experiences had sintered them together into a single hardened metal tool. The formed connection conducted between them the sorrow, and hope, in each. Still, there was a difference between them. The hope of Selene and Nike was pure and powerful. The hope of Samson and Elio was not for themselves, but for a promising future they could help to start.

The fire consumed itself past the point of raging now. It just smoldered in a dangerous heat in front of them. It emitted little smoke, or indication of its heat, but they all knew it was potent. Perhaps fires are mesmerizing because they are a progress of degradation, of returning something to a less complex form, its original form. In the smoldering coals are the components of the past.

Elio broke the silence. "Will you follow me tomorrow?" he said while handing everyone a single crescent coin, except for Selene, to whom he gave three.

They each nodded.

They were all tired and soon were resting. Samson was one of the last to fall asleep, as his mind was still churning on a lifetime of thoughts.

The storm,

destroyed the coast,

and dug

a spiraling blade

deep into the inland,

filling lakes

swamps and rivers;

releasing leaves,

and cracking branches,

to fall into

the raging currents,

flowing

to the now settled

ocean.

Chapter 22: The Exiled

"So what do we do with these two?" asked Nike, examining the two guards, now conscious but still in pain and weighted by their injuries.

"They were saying some nasty things," commented Samson.

Selene came up close to them and unsheathed her shiny knife. The orange and red sunrise gleamed on the blade. "We don't kill unless it's absolutely necessary." She then cut the rope binding them to a post in the shack. She then took a thick handmade rope and tied them, loosely back to post, but the knots were out of their reach. She then found a small dull butter knife and gave it to the one with the dark beard.

"This should keep them occupied for a while," she said. She then went and used the knife to cut the electrical wires of the telegraph machine.

"Ok then, let's go," Nike commanded.

They grabbed their already packed bags. Earlier in the morning they had confirmed their plan. Elio had mapped out the compound, and the others had formulated a strategy. They would attack a weapons storage area and ignite the gun powder manufacturing facilities. They would also steal as much of the explosives as they could carry to possibly detonate and disable the boats in a nearby marine. Then, during the confusion they would confiscate a boat and take it to the island. That was the plan.

The four now walked along the highway, but they planned to take cover in the foliage of the next island once they had crossed the marsh. Several peninsulas and barrier islands were separated from the mainland by the marsh. The attackers were on the first island at the end of the marsh and the causeway. The island with the lighthouse was then across another bridge between the islands, but the islanders had brought down the bridge.

Another tortoise was crossing the road ahead of them. Samson noticed that this one had a peculiar deformation on its shell. One of its shell plates was smooth and transparent, like a window into its innards. Samson went to pick him up. Like the other one, he opened his sharp mouth wide. Selene came up next to him.

"This mutation is from the Fall. Most of the animals and people that had random deformations from the quantum entanglement have already perished, but this guy has made it. I knew these tortoise's had long lives, but they must also be very hardy," remarked Samson.

"It doesn't seem to have affected his disposition," said Selene.

"Well, he has had a long and trying life…" Samson said as he brushed away his white curly hair from his right ear. The hair revealed a mangled lobe and helix, or top of the ear. The parts appeared perforated along the edges, almost like the light rays emitting from a source.

"I thought I had seen something, but assumed it was an injury," explained Selene.

"Well, it's just the way it is. It doesn't really matter in the scheme of things…and this guy has kept on despite it as well," he said as he placed the tortoise on the edge of the road. The tortoise took a quick bite at Samson's foot, but did little damage. Samson pointed toward a large matching hole in the ground lower down the slope from the road. Selene smiled. They caught up to the others and continued on.

It took them a good part of the day to cross on the road. The sun was lowering when they could see the edge of the marsh ahead, and the formation of an island. Old battered houses and docks lined the marsh nearby. The unkempt structures were missing planks and pilings, and many no longer had a clear channel to the ocean.

The four began to crouch on the outer slopes of the causeway, two on each side. They would then surround the weapons area from two sides. They slipped into the thick foliage of mangroves and scrub brush. They had to push and slash their way through it. Selene and Elio went to the left and Samson and Nike went to the right.

Samson watched as first Elio and then Selene disappeared into the engulfing brush. He then turned and followed Nike. The ground was wet, so each footstep sunk into the decaying matter. Samson meticulously planned each step. He dodged small branches or dry leaves that could crack and emit noise. As he walked, he slowly drew the knife Selene had given to him and readied his slingshot in an open pocket.

Nike and Samson noticed little sign of any man's presence yet. Then the thick brush opened up to a canopy of ancient oak trees. A corpse hung from a noose in the middle of the opening. The body had not yet fully decomposed, and leathery skin and tendons still held the exposed bones together. Then the sea breeze engaged. The bones rattled softly—a morbid wind chime.

Nike looked back to Samson and nodded forward. As they were about to leave the clearing, the wind rushed in again and one of the hanging body's feet liberated itself and fell to the ground in a thud. They both paused and looked at each other for a few moments. They heard nothing else but the indigenous sounds of nature.

A worn path lead away from the clearing, but they both knew not to take it, as it might be guarded or watched. Instead, they left the clearing barely in view of the path, but close enough that they could follow its general direction.

It did not take long for glimpses of a white structure to appear from the crevices between the leaves. Samson became more cautious, and tried to align himself behind the trunks of large trees on his way to the structure. Upon closer inspection, the structure was not a pristine white. Moss, mold and lichen had grown on the white surfaces. Green mold had created curved shapes on the structure. A little more growth would have created an effective camouflage in the woods.

Samson surveyed the area from behind a juniper tree. No one was guarding the area, unless they were hiding inside the window-less structure. It was large enough to conceal a dozen men.

Nike had also drew out his knife and was behind a nearby juniper tree. The common juniper's presence, a type of cedar tree, meant that the ground was saturated with salt and sand. He pointed to the structure and began to count with his fingers. On five they would storm the structure. He closed each finger individually until only his fist was left.

They both rushed up to the back side of the structure and kicked in a flimsy aluminum door. Six old personal 4 wheeled off-road vehicles lay dormant inside. Samson went to one and observed the settled dust on the seat and tires.

"These don't look like they've been used recently," whispered Samson.

Nike unscrewed the lid off one of the gas tanks and peered inside.

"Dry as a bone," Nike muttered.

"I don't see any tanks lying around neither," confirmed Samson.

A deep pop suddenly echoed through the forest and into the structure.

"That's a gunshot," remarked Samson, no longer whispering.

"Must be the others. We gotta go help," suggested Nike.

"Yes, but we don't want to rush in and make things worse. Let's still be cautious," said Samson.

Another pop rang out. Nike ran from the structure without waiting another second.

"Wait, dammit!" Samson said in the loudest voice he could muster without yelling.

Nike was gone and only his galloping footsteps through the leaves was audible.

"Crap," Samson muttered to himself as he exited the building and took out his slingshot. To the left of the door Nike was running down a clear path in the thicket. He was far ahead, and Samson knew there was no way he could ever catch the speed of a younger athlete.

Samson began to walk down the path at a slower pace than Nike, but he was not as cautious as he had been in the woods. He searched through his pockets and pulled out the lone crescent coin. He placed it snuggly in the pouch of his sling shot. Another shot rang out. The sound vibrated through the twisted wood of the trees and his bones. He took heavy breaths. His feet crushed the dry fallen leaves as he ran.

Ahead on the path, concrete barracks appeared in front of Nike. The mortar between the concrete blocks was cracked and decayed. This resulted in the structures looking unstable and more like the crumbling ruins of a medieval castle. Old crates were stacked everywhere. A group of a dozen people carrying firearms and other weapons stood around two kneeling people, Selene and Elio. Nearby on the ground were two dead bodies that appeared to have been shot.

Nike reached the group first and attacked their fray like a fierce whirling storm. His arms slashed and fell several of the people on the outside of the group. They tumbled like trees under the rain and wind of a hurricane. However, just as the hurricane loses power as it crawls onto land, Nike's blows began to slow, and became more defensive. Several of those guarding Selene and Elio had been distracted by the attack, and Selene and Elio took the opportunity to rise. They also brought several of the men down near to them, but were soon once again the center of attention. A few shots from smoking firearms began to ring out again.

Samson pulled back the crescent coin in the pouch and stretched the slingshot bands to a point of nearly breaking. He aimed. His fingers released. The disk flew true and a spurt of blood spouted from the cranium of a man raising a rifle near Selene and Elio. He fell to the ground, and others in the group now noticed the old man closing in on them from the path. More shots weren't fired because the people near Selene, Elio and Nike were occupied with close combat and did not have time to reload their weapons. That action would result in a knife slash to the body.

Samson spotted several rocks on the path ahead and reached down to grab one. Then everything went black...

Bones
and darkness
do not arrive
on a ship
flying black colors
but on the sharp edge
of a sheathed sword.

Chapter 23: One Horn

Samson opened his eyes to the cool morning air. His skull hurt. He tilted his head toward his left to observe his surroundings. He was lying on a hard, cold and cracked concrete slab. His hands were tied together. How had that happened?

Circling him were people who had the appearance of worn guerrilla fighters holding a variety of weapons and firearms. The figures held dented rifles and handguns with scratched and peeling paint. A dark spectrum of clothing hung on their thin bodies, but they all seemed to be wearing black fabric tied around their right biceps. They stood around three other tied up figures—a sleek tan man who seemed to still hold himself tall, a scarred man who also showed strength, but was clearly weary, and a young girl, whose face shed light onto the darkness around her. "Who were they?" he wondered.

Behind the soldiers stood an Adirondack-style lean-to structure, or essentially three concrete walls with a roof. Under the roof lay wooden crates holding stacks of identical cylindrical objects.

The back of his skull throbbed. He tilted his head slowly in the opposite direction to his right. There lie another man. A trail of dried blood went from his forehead to a puddle on the ground. The man emitted no breath and the open eyes had lost their glimmer. Samson wondered who had done this, not knowing he had.

"The old man's awake!" one of the ragged armed men yelled. "Go get Haden!" Another younger man ran off on a path.

Samson forced himself up. His knife and slingshot were gone. As soon as he stood up, a rusted barrel met his face.

"Where you goin' old man?" Samson looked blankly at him in response. Seemed like he had heard that many times before, but could not recall where. Come to think of it, he could not remember much of anything.

The other kneeling men and the girl looked toward him and appeared to show some sympathy. Did he know them? It seemed like to him that they were clearly on the wrong side of this conflict.

Samson said the only thing that came to his mind, "What did he do to deserve that?" he said looking at the dead man lying next to him.

"What the hell's wrong with you?" exclaimed the scrawny man holding the corroded rifle.

"I bet that gun doesn't even shoot," replied Samson without giving his words any thought before saying them. Was he always this aggressive? His subconscious seemed to be looking for a fight.

"Good grief. That's no gunshot. There's a coin stuck in his head from a slingshot. *Your* slingshot."

What? Had he really killed that man? Didn't seem like something he would do, or did it? Something intricately hard and sharp grew inside him.

Suddenly, from around the corner of the path the man had run down previously, several others appeared. Their presence caused whatever structure was inside him to harden. The suction of their presence felt like blood being drawn from his internal organs. But it also tightened his muscles and the adrenaline seemed to anesthetize the welt on the back of his head.

"I'd tighten your lips. Time to meet Haden," exclaimed the man.

Four men had emerged on the path. One was taller, and based on his posture, appeared to Samson to be some sort of leader. Those surrounding him looked similar to the others he had seen. Their clothing was tattered, and some had blood stains. They were also heavily armed.

The taller man wore a black suit jacket. The jacket was rough around the edges, and its darkness also contrasted with smudges of dust and dirt that had collected on its fabric. The man wearing it walked sternly and confidently. His skin was leathered from the sun. His hair had also started to whiten, but had only conquered about half of his scalp. His naturally dark hair intermixed with the white hair, but concentrated near his temples and on his facial hair. His beard was well trimmed around his angular face. His eyes were almost black, as the brown in his eyes was very dark. On his head he wore an old pirate hat. The kind you would have found in a coastal tourist store, but the younger followers probably had no idea of this. To the man's benefit, the hat was also well worn and the skull and cross bones on the front had peeled off, leaving one eye of the skull gone and the bones severed.

Regardless, the man cast a dark shadow. Samson, instinctively clinched his fists.

"Well behold, four little wholesome beacons of light," said the man in the dirty black coat, but as he observed Samson and smelled him, he said, "well maybe three." The man looked at the others surrounding them and at the body lying next to Samson. He gave a smile that sneered on one side.

Removing the hat, and revealing a grotesque growth, the man continued, "Where are my manners? Allow me to introduce myself. These folks call me Haden. Maybe I should change it to Hades. For some reason, they've chosen to answer to me."

On Haden's head protruded a sharp sickle shaped bone from the left side. Samson thought it resembled a horn, like what a demon would have on both sides of his head. The protrusion was an unusual feature that had not always been there. Haden appeared to recognize the reaction everyone had in seeing it. He stood for a moment, allowing everyone to examine the horn.

"By the looks of you, I bet you plan on making your way to that island across the way, the one with the lighthouse. Well, you don't need to be worried. They aren't taking anymore. They even demolished the bridge onto the island. The only way is by boat. You know how to sail? I doubt a group of pilgrimming landlubbers would." Haden paused for a bit, and gazed upon the face of each visitor. Samson was perplexed by this man.

The stacked crates were open, and exposing tattered sticks of dynamite. It looked like they may have been handmade from a combination of old and newly synthesized materials. Each had a twisted fuse ready to ignite. How long each fuse would burn before detonation was uncertain. The open crates were in between himself and the other three kneeling individuals, but closer to himself.

Samson still struggled to recall what he was doing in this place and who those other three were. They seemed to share some comradery with himself, but he had no idea why. His gut told him that the current situation was dire. And then there was this grotesque looking man standing in front of him. The man was not necessarily grotesque from the horn. Rather, a grim and dark energy swirled around Haden.

"I've heard that you have not shown us kindness in your visit. You see, we knew you were comin'. You cut our line with those two out on the causeway. That is not just a communication line, but an alarm system. We noticed that the line was cut because the electric circuit was broken.

So now the question is what do we do with you?" Do with us? Samson did not know how to respond. He searched his memories. The last thing he could recall was sitting in the cramped compartment of a commercial jet airliner. He closed his eyes.

Samson remembered wearing a well-worn sport coat and slacks. He was returning from a business trip in San Jose, California, the revered cradle of modern electronic technology. Even then, with the planes flying faster than the speed of sound on the edge of space, the journey across the continent took time. The chairs on the plane were cramped together as to maximize the profits of the airline. They did provide entertainment in the form of virtual movies.

The passenger next to him was a young girl. She had a large virtual reality headset covering her eyes and ears with a shiny blue plastic material. A blue light glowed from the device near the girl's temple. The light signified that the headset was connected to the planes wireless entertainment system.

The girl nodded and smiled in response to whatever she was watching. In the seat on the other side of the girl was her mother. She did not look familiar to Samson, although she also wore one of the headsets that covered her eyes and ears. They had no relation to himself and were merely fellow passengers on this flight.

In the real world, the horned man's boots clicked on the concrete in front of Samson. The man said, "You do realize that murder like this would be punishable by death on your beloved island?"

Samson continued to remember. He looked around the flight, and nearly everyone was wearing the headsets and effectively shielded from the sights and sounds around them. He opened the opaque shade of the window next to his seat. The night sky was dark. Far below, the bright straight lines and sharp angles of man and his cities glowed. The black earth was illuminated by a grid of electricity. For a moment it appeared peaceful. And then it happened. A few scattered explosions began to illuminate small specks below. Their number began to multiply, leaving an even distribution of fires on the ground below. His right ear bled. A scream rang out behind him.

"So...who do we hang first?" The voice in front of him said in the present world. The sound of the boots softened as they left the concrete to the soft soil.

Samson's shoulder reddened with blood. He remembered turning and scanning across the rows of the seats on the plane. Several of the passengers' bodies had appeared to self-destruct into a still corpse. The process was fast but horrifying. Their flesh would change color and distort in a random manner. Others were writhing in pain. Only 20 or so of the 200 passengers appeared unharmed. Within their secluded digital worlds, they did not even notice the decay of life around them.

A flight attendant, dressed in a crimson uniform raced through the aisle, apparently assessing the situation. He went to Samson. "Sir, I think the pilots are also ill, but the door to the cockpit is locked, can you help me force it open? Is your ear ok?" Samson nodded twice and rose from his seat. He had to push his way past the body of the girl next to him, still healthy, but lost in the digital entertainment of her headset, and then the deceased body of her mother.

Samson and the flight attendant rushed toward the front of the plane. The door to the cockpit was made of polished aluminum, with an aluminum handle. The locked door would not be easy to open.

The flight attendant commented, "The plane has an effective autopilot, but we still need to make sure the controls are set correctly." The attendant opened a nearly hidden compartment on the wall and reached far back into it.

The attendant explained, "They do leave this hidden tool to help us get in, if needed, but it really needs two people to use it." He pulled out an aluminum tool that looked something like a crowbar, but was designed to fit in between the edge of the door and the frame near to the lock.

"Here you grab the handle and turn and pull, while I force it with this." The attendant inserted the tool and applied his body weight as leverage. Samson took the handle and leaned back to pull the door open. It took a few moments, but the tool had opened the bolt back just enough that the door started to slide open. The bolt scratched across the metal frame and let out a screech. Then the door opened.

The two entered the cockpit. In the dark, red and white indicators glowed all around them. The two pilots were both dead. One had hunched over onto the controls. Her body had pushed the steering wheel forward. They could not see much now out the front windshield.

The attendant went to the hunched over pilot on the left and examined the indicators. He looked at the altimeter and then exclaimed, "Oh no." A few moments later the columns of many trees emerged from the fog ahead of them.

An object suddenly cracked against his head. He fell uncontrolled to the ground. Laying his head sideways on the ground, his eyes opened.

"Samson!" exclaimed the girl. He suddenly knew the voice. The boots of Haden were but a few inches from his head. He recalled everything.

"We might not even need to hang this one. He's already half dead," Haden remarked as he kicked Samson in the stomach. Samson curled up and moved his sight to the others that he once again recognized. He knew they had to get out of there. About a dozen of the capturers surrounded them. Their only real option was to run. Samson looked over at Nike, Elio, and Selene and nodded to them.

Suddenly, Elio erupted from his knees. They should have tied his hands, because in a few quick motions he had grabbed a rifle from a scrawny man nearby and used its butt and ammunition to take out three of the captors. The first man received the butt of the rifle to his forehead, and two others gunshots to their chests.

Samson snapped. The strength he had in his age was deceiving, and now adrenaline magnified it. He used his arms to sweep out Haden's legs. As Haden fell to the ground, Samson swiftly removed the sword from Haden's side and thrashed around himself, clearing a radius. He ran to the others.

Elio did not succeed in surprising the other men. He was in close contact with a large man. They were fighting over the control of another rifle.

As Samson ran toward them, crossed by one of the containers containing the cylindrical objects. They were explosives…maybe dynamite. He instinctively grabbed several of them. "Let's go!" he yelled at Selene and Nike, who although was initially stunned, had now joined the fight. Selene used a quick maneuver to take control of one of the captor's knives. She then stuck it deep into the gut of the man. Nike simply over powered a man near him and in a few punches sent him to the ground. They began to turn and run toward Samson.

A blunt pop echoed out. Elio fell to the ground, blood running from his head. Selene screamed, "Elio!" Samson grabbed her arm and they ran into the woods.

A sharp pain stung Samson's side, but he did not look down. The three ran at full speed away from the structure. Ahead they could see the landscape behind the trees turn to blue. Samson worried for a moment that their captures would trap them on the beach.

"There!' Nike said. A collection of old wooden docks and marine vehicles emerged ahead.

Samson reached into his pockets and found his lighter. With two clicks he lit the fuse of one of the cylinders as he ran. Selene's eyes widened as she watched him do this. Samson tossed the explosive behind them.

As they reached the coast, the explosion sent light shockwaves against their backs. The waves seemed to push them forward. Samson pointed to a small sailboat at the end of the dock. Its sails were lowered, but left on the mast. A few other vessels had motors, but looked unmaintained, and the several other sailboats were not fitted.

Samson glanced back and several of the captors were still close behind them. Their six feet now pounded on the wooden dock. The long dock extended out over shallow water and grass to a deep channel. Samson lit another cylinder. As they came closer to the chosen sailboat, he threw the cylinder behind them onto the dock. It rocked on the old planks and stopped. They arrived at the boat and jumped in.

Selene cut the mooring lines holding the vessel to the dock with the knife she had stolen. The knife cut through the old lines with ease, and embedded into the wood below. Samson dropped three more of the explosives and Haden's sword into the hull and quickly began to hoist the mainsail by pulling on the halyard running to a pulley at the top of the mast. The other two watched toward the dock and the captors now running on the planks.

The fuse met its end and the explosive sent splinters in all directions. The three ducked instinctively. The explosion had not injured any of the captors, but left an impassible gap in the dock and damaged several of the other vessels. The captors one by one reached the damage until one arrived with a rifle and began to take aim at the escapees.

Nike kicked the boat away from the dock. The boat barely had enough space for all three of them. Its hull sunk deep into the water. They slowly drifted into the channel, as Samson continued to raise the sail.

A hole exploded on the sail a foot from Samson's head. The captor holding the rifle took aim again, but missed them completely with the second shot. The sail was up, but the sail and boom were limp, acting as a flag in the wind.

Samson fell to the stern of the boat and took control of the line attached to the boom. He pulled it in and with his other hand directed the boat away from the dock using a wooden tiller. As he reached an optimal alignment with the wind, the boat surged forward. They were at an angle diagonal from the dock, but making good speed.

Samson tied secure the lines to hold their course. Haden now stood at the edge of the splintered dock. Haden crossed his arms and gave them a grimacing stare. Nike raised Haden's sword in defiance.

Selene came to Samson's side and touched his arm. Samson had been shot. The bullet had impacted the side of his torso. His blood had already spilled out into the white fiberglass of the boat. It had trickled between the textures of the unfinished material and formed intricate arms and branches. They appeared to Samson as a red fractal reef of coral.

"That's peculiar," he remarked. Once his mind realized his injury, he sunk deep into the hull of the boat.

Selene tore the sleeve off the shirt she was wearing a pressed it hard against the wound. The red seeped in the fabric and more blots of coral expanded. "There. Hold on old man."

Samson gave the tiller to Nike and pointed toward the horizon. They had taken a course with the wind rushing over the front of the port side of the boat. He hoped that they could simply hold this course and not need to turn the boat's bow to reach their destination. The boat skated on a widening inter-coastal waterway. The water roughened only slightly by the wind.

Samson's lifted his head to the back over the stern of the boat. Farther down the waterway stood the charred remnants of one of the bridges that had been detonated, just as Haden had said. No other boats followed them.

The salty but soft sea air flowed through Samson's hair. It had been a long time since he been on a boat like this. He was losing consciousness. He corrected the tautness of the sail a few times. Clearly, Nike had little seafaring experience. His body relaxed more into the curve of the boat's hull. Moving his sight across the bow, a sliver soon appeared ahead of them on the horizon.

"Samson, it's the lighthouse!" exclaimed Selene. Then looked down to the foaming seawater she said, "But Elio, and now you. You must hold on."

Samson passed out.

He soon dreamt of words.

>Even after
>the column of brick
>has fallen into rubble,
>the light it emitted
>above the waves
>will continue on.

Chapter 24: Half a Day

Samson opened his eyes to warm, moist air. He lay in a small white room, upon a comfortable bed. Selene was by his side. Haden's sword leaned against a white wall. One side of the blade was straight, while the other curved to the tip. Black leather covered the hilt below a battered metal guard. Its blade was beaten, but sharp.

"I knew you would pull through," she thanked.

Light from the outside danced between palm branches before landing on dust floating in the room. Based on the light's source, Samson could tell it was mid-morning.

"How long?" he asked.

"Just two days."

He looked down to his side where he had been shot. Hand crafted paper and bandages of woven plant fibers covered his wound. A thick brown paste had been layered between the bandage and his innards.

"Its ground tree bark, mixed with honey. They said it would help coagulation and stop the blood. And honey is antibacterial."

Several stitches below the paste stretched and plowed against his skin as he breathed. All things considered, he felt relatively good.

Selene picked a cup crafted from wavy glass, and filled with water. "It's still a little salty. They have a small desalination machine." He drank it.

Another middle aged woman dressed in a wrapping of burlap-like material marched into the room. She introduced herself, "I'm Philomena and the acting doctor here. You should be grateful of the path of the bullet. It missed everything important. You should make a full recovery. You also seem to be healing rapidly. I thought that you might have had some work done, since you were from the time before descent."

'Descent,' it reminded him again of the plane crash, and his abrupt introduction to the new world. He had undergone the age reduction procedures that were common to most individuals of the time. He looked to Selene, and then to the doctor, and nodded his head. He then noticed a beautiful silver necklace around Philomena's beck. The long jewel was weighted on Philomena's chest by a broche made of a complex intertwining of curved silver wires.

Samson closed his eyes, and put his energy into raising his back from the soft bed. For a moment his mind was thrown back to when he awoke amid a shattered forest. The wreckage of the airplane was all around him, smoldering. Bodies lay limp around him. Some were deformed from the infliction of entanglement, and others were cut apart, just like the vehicle. He remembered his body, dirty, bloody, but intact. He recalled the pain, and then the endorphins kicking in. In the white infirmary he was now sitting up.

"Don't rush it. Healing takes time," warned Philomena.

Samson's side ached, but mildly compared to previous injuries. He threw his legs over the side of the bed, and his feet landed with a thud on an old tile floor. He stood up.

"Let's see this place," he said to both of them. They were clearly in no position to argue.

They brought him new, clean clothing. The course woven fabric appeared mostly handmade by the people of the island. The fabric was cotton and dyed in strange colorful patterns. His old jacket hung on the back of the chair near to the bed. After he put the new clothes on, he put his familiar jacket on over them.

Samson began to walk out toward the door. He stumbled a bit. Selene offered to help, but he brushed her away.

They walked to the open door together. A bright light emitted from the sunlit gardens outside. Samson's and Selene's shadows blocked the sun from the tile floor as they left the building. Philomena followed behind them.

Once outside, Samson cupped his hand over his eyes and looked toward the sun. The energy emitted filled him and cleansed him. To his opposite side the lighthouse rose above the foliage. The brick pinnacle stood about 100 yards away from him, and its wick was unlit in the sunlight.

A lush garden of edible fruits and vegetables extended out in all directions. The boundaries of the garden were paths that crept out as flowing veins. They connected the buildings together in optimal routes that were worn into the ground. Growing in the garden were tomato plants, carrot tops, squash, potatoes, peanuts, blueberry and blackberry bushes and many herbs and spices. Above the plants and in the centers of the gardens rose banana trees, peach trees, and even a few pecan trees in the distance. It reminded him of an antique image of the original garden, the one called Eden.

Selene knelt to a short sunflower near the back edge of one of the gardens. She touched its leaves and petals gently. Bee's landed and departed from the flowers round seed filled core. "Beautiful flower," said Samson.

"Yes. It's the same as one's we grew in pots," replied Selene. Was this the same type of plant she had left by the burnt out house, now far away? He knew that this land had never been touched by the enhancement of quantum entanglement, but despite this, these people had cultivated every available area of land.

Samson felt a light pat on his shoulder. He looked over, but was not startled. He was more at ease here than he had been anywhere since the Fall. The red reef and defenses within him had fallen deep below the sea of his soul.

He gazed at a beautiful woman with joyous wrinkles and long white hair. She appeared to be approximately the same age as himself. A purple handmade ribbon held her long hair together on her back. She wore a robe dyed in a random but structured pattern of black and white. Her delicate but deceivingly strong hands held a bamboo walking stick that was about the same height as she was.

She spoke, "I heard that you were awake. It appears that you are ready for a proper tour."

Samson, looked to Selene, who smiled and nodded. She leaned to Samson and whispered, "She's the leader."

The woman smiled. "I am Theia. Welcome to what we have renamed the island of Rhodes and the village of Alexandria. Selene tells me that it has been a long journey here. Perhaps longest for you." He did not recognize the woman anywhere in his memories, but the way she talked was solidifying and soothing.

"You need this more than I," Theia said as she handed Samson the bamboo walking stick.

"Thank you. I am glad we made it, but have also lost several along the way. I am sure Selene told you about the loss of your own, Rhodus. We also lost her...her soulmate, Elio. Did Selene tell you about their village?"

"Yes, in your sleep we had a lot of time to talk. We had heard of other places rising up recently. I was sad to learn about the fate of their village. But you are here now. Shall we? I suppose that you've already seen the Place of Healing." Samson nodded in agreement. They walked down a path leaving straight from the white building where he awoke.

"Where's Nike?" he whispered to Selene.

"He's fine. You'll see him soon," She replied. "Pay attention, it is amazing."

The path soon led to an active area with many people walking, talking and working. This appeared to be the center of the village. The path was lined with shops for various crafts, such as a blacksmith and carpenter, but adjacent to them was what appeared to be an electrical shop.

Beyond it stood a machine shop capable of fabricating metal parts. A bakery also filled the air with an interesting aroma. The scent was not that of a wheat bread bakery, but of other ingredients such as coconut.

"This is the center of Alexandria. The 'higher' technologies were on equal grounds as the more primitive ones. One must realize that all trades are valuable and none are of greater importance than another. Still, they each have value, and we use trade and commerce to obtain what each needs," explained Theia.

Samson admired the artisans immersed in each of their crafts. The blades of the blacksmith glimmered in the sun in front of a smoldering kiln. Nearby, with another kiln in the background, a potter molded containers from a thick red clay on a spinning table wheel. The container started as a body of clay, with no recognizable structure or form. Its surface was undulated and random. The potter stepped on a peddle that caused the wheel and mass to slowly spin. The potter's hands first began to give the mass of clay a symmetry about the center of the wheel. The potter then began to dig into the center of the clay from the top, creating an empty space within it.

"Only a hollow pot can carry water," remarked Selene. Samson recognized that the hollowness behind the once ragged red reef of his being had been slowly filling for some time. In addition, fluids existed there that had long been forgotten. He was remembering the sweet taste of wine crafted for love, the excitement of black coffee, and the balance of tea. He craved a cup of his yaupon tea that he had crafted time and again in the morning next to a dying campfire.

Samson noticed a hut upon whose walls, window sills, and roof overhangs hung drying leaves and beans. When he arrived at the front of the hut with Theia and Selene behind him, a man came out and handed him an intricately crafted tea cup displaying swirls of red and blue pigment. It had probably been made by the potter across the street. The tea artisan brought a large pot and poured the contents into the cup in Samson's hand. Samson took a sip and was filled with the warmth and complexity of a tea mixed with a balance of native plants. The liquid tasted of hibiscus, black tea, and citrus. The man encouraged Samson to take the tea with him on the tour.

"It's good, but you have any Yaupin?" The tea artisan nodded in reply.

"Watch out!"

A ball made of crudely laced together plant fabric landed by his feet. A group of a dozen or so children of various ages swarmed up around him. They were laughing and giggling. Following close behind was Nike.

"Making a comeback I see," remarked Samson.

"Maybe in a different sport," replied Nike. Nike's eyes were bright, showing contentment and joy. His body played in sport so naturally with the children, but now it was for fun instead of glory. Nike stopped for a moment next to Samson, Theia and Selene, still rolling the ball in his hands. He signaled to the children to run far out for a catch.

"If only Ares could have made it here," thought Nike out loud.

"Indeed, there are many that should be here with us."

Theia appeared to notice this moment of solace and motioned to Samson. "I want you to know, they will not be forgotten, and neither will those of the past," explained Theia. Nike threw the crudely made ball and went running after it toward the swarm of children.

Theia brought them around to different parts of the island. They toured the living spaces of the people. Engineers explained the workings of the electric power generator and the water desalination plant. The facilities had been engineered from a combination of repaired parts from before the Fall, and new ingenious handcrafted components. Metal and organic mechanisms seemed to work together in harmony.

They then went to a small building with a small sign saying "Library." The three entered. Book shelves filled every available space. Most of the books appeared worn and yellowed. Some were even missing a cover, exposing the binding. Electrical lights emitted from a device in the middle of the room. Next to it loomed a large glass cabinet. Within it stood stacks of thousands of the small transparent information cubes glimmering in blue light. Theia signaled to Samson and Selene to follow her to this machine.

"We have done our best to collect as many of these bits of information as possible. Luckily, they are nearly indestructible. You are welcome to try it out." Something inside Samson told him not to.

"I was there, as I think you were too, I do not need to see it this way," explained Samson. Selene accepted the invitation though, and sat down at the console. A vivid screen illuminated and displayed a menu.

"Here," said Theia. She placed a device on Selene's head. Immediately the items on the menu changed colors indicating that Selene had selected them with her mind. Soon displayed on the screen were people enjoying themselves on a beach, which looked similar to nearby coastlines. Some swam in the crashing waves. Others built detailed sandcastles, and others just sat in drooping chairs while snacking on neatly packaged food and sipping on colorful cylindrical drinks.

"They all looked so happy," commented Selene.

"They are on vacation. That is what this place used to be. It has now shifted its purpose, but we still have managed to maintain some of that light and hope," added Theia.

"Who were the friendly chaps we met across the channel?" asked Samson.

"Ah yes, many of them were once part of our community. However, they broke the laws we have in place. They were then exiled for their crimes. Now they seemed to have made it their goal to seek some sort of revenge," answered Theia. An image of Haden appeared in Samson's mind, with his single asymmetrical horn.

"But we are connected with them, and with all of this age. We are connected in more than one way." Theia brushed aside some of the white hair covering her forehead and above her right temple and ear. A shiny material reflected the light from the digitally displayed images that Selene was still viewing. The skin of Theia's face stopped in a rounded pattern, like a beach around a silvery lake. The lake was some sort of metal material, but was obviously not engineered by man, and appeared biological. The scrambling of quantum entanglement had caused this change. Samson lightly brushed his hand past her face and smiled.

"Come, I want to conclude this tour properly," Theia said. She led them out of the library and down a path toward the lighthouse. She flipped a switch on the wall as the entered the tower. It had been a long time since Samson had seen anyone do that. They all climbed up its old cast iron spiral stairs toward its pinnacle. The stairs had been damaged by rust and corrosion, but were now painted over with a thick black tar. Samson still held the cup of tea gently as he climbed the stairs, being careful not to spill what little remained.

Soon they reached the circular balcony at the top. The lighthouse was lit by a collection of bright LEDs in front of a polished mirror that rotated slowly around to point toward every portion of the horizon. It blinded them when it crossed their position, so they all quickly turned to look outward.

Theia began to speak, "This is our signal to the world. We are here. We will accept you."

"Unless you break the rules," corrected Samson.

"But they are very simple and fair. All within the coast of this island must treat others as they wish to be treated. You cannot take something that is not given to you or traded properly, whether that is tea or life."

The three looked out from the lighthouse toward the Atlantic Ocean on one side of the island. The waves crashed rhythmically onto the beach. From this height one could also see the flowing and swirling patterns that the waves had carved into the sand along the coast.

The peaceful grandeur of the ocean swept over all three and energized their souls. Samson couldn't help but think that if someday historians and archeologists would mark the ruins of this place as the kernel of a new world and society. They would be dusting off the artifacts and contemplating their usage and meaning, and probably characterizing them with purposes that were never intended. But that would only happen if they succeeded.

The peace broke. The sound of a metal bell rang out over the tree canopy and gardens of the island and up to the three on the lighthouse.

"Oh no,' exclaimed Theia as she raced around the rail of the balcony to the side facing the mainland. The channel that they had crossed to escape the exiled people was clearly visible. Faraway they could also see the crumbling bridges of grey concrete. In the distance, a plume of white smoke caught Samson's eye.

The smoke was coming from what appeared to be a struggle near the bridge. But then something more frightening appeared upon the water. The dirty gray sails and masts of a large sailboat appeared on the water. The vessel headed toward the island with its sails pulled tight to capture the power of the sea breeze.

Samson recognized what this meant. He looked at Theia and then at Selene, who were also looking at the smoke and boat approaching in the distance.

"Where is the boat we arrived on, and the explosives?" asked Samson.

"What explosives?" asked Theia.

Selene opened her jacket and pulled out from an inner pocket the remaining handmade cylinders of explosives, along with the same lighter Samson had picked up at the store where he had first encountered Selene. She handed them to Samson and then pointed toward several docks not far from the lighthouse on the channel side of the island. The small sailboat they had used was there tethered to a dock. Samson stuffed the explosives and lighter into his jacket. He left the balcony without a word and raced down the spirals of the stairs. His feet met only some of the steps and skipped over many others. Several times he almost fell.

"Wait!" Selene exclaimed behind him. He went on and reached the ground floor. He exited the lighthouse and ran down a path in the direction of the docks. They were not far away and soon he arrived at them and to the small sailboat. In a nearby fishing boat he spotted fishing poles and a spear gun leaning against the hull. He quickly grabbed the spear gun, powered by a stiff rubber band.

The sails of the small boat were still rigged and the mainsail was neatly secured to the mast. Samson leaped onto the boat and it rocked under his weight. His hand unraveled the rope that spiraled around the main sail. Soon the rigging was ready for his departure. He felt a tug on the back of his shirt. It was Selene.

"Samson! It's not time yet," she said.

"Yes it is. You know it is. It must be me. Stay here. Your journey will continue with them." He hugged her from the boat while she stood on the dock. Their heads were at eye level since the boat was floating lower in the water. He dug in his pocket and pulled out the folded paper he had written on a few nights before. He gave it to Selene. She untied the bowline of the boat and he untied the stern.

Tears trailed from Selene's eyes as Samson pushed away from the dock. He smiled at her. She forced a smile back at him

Samson directed his attention to piloting the vessel. He raised the main sail and tied off the halyard onto a cleat. He then adjusted his course away from the dock. The wind filled the sails and they ruffled with noise. Samson adjusted them to a nearly optimal position and they became quiet. The boat gained speed. With only one passenger, the little hull was faster than before.

This reminded him of his teenage years in Florida, and sailing a similar small craft across waters just as these on weekends. He smiled at the memory. More memories also came flooding back. He recalled taking his children out on the same small boat. They often did not appreciate the slow but steady progress of the small vessel, but he had hoped they would appreciate it one day. Did they ever have that chance? He remembered sailing out to a small island with them where they would find washed up shells on the beach.

His mind returned to the task at hand. The two masts of Haden's ship protruded above the bow of Samson's small craft. It would not take long for their paths to once again cross. A strong gust of sea breeze rushed in and the small boat rose higher in the water and gained speed. The larger ship ahead tilted under the gust of wind as well. He held the tiller tight, but his hands were shaking.

Samson looked back at the island to a view of two figures standing on the balcony of the lighthouse. He imagined Selene opening the paper, finding the glimmering information storage cubes, and reading the graphite marks. She would leave the three remaining crescent coins still jingling in her pocket. The cubes contained pictures and videos of his family. He had not viewed them since before the Fall. In graphite, the words on the paper read:

You are the moon.
Use your gravity
to guide the tides
to reform the landscape
in gentle floods
and cutting rivers.

The larger sailing ship came upon him. Perspective left his mind, and it appeared as though the bow sprit was towering over his vessel when they were hundreds of yards away. He stabilized his course by tying off the tiller with a loose line of rope. He then drew out the explosives and used another bit of rope to lash them together by wrapping them over and over again. He also twisted there fuses together.

The large approaching ship had been repaired over the decades in many spots. Dark regions splotched the hull where patches of carbon were epoxied over weak areas and faults. No effort was made in making the repairs aesthetically pleasing. On the top deck of the ship several larger weapons had also been mounted. This included the many barrels of the decedent of a Gatlin gun, the larger lateral barrel of a smaller cannon and a mortar barrel pointed to the sky protruded from the deck. Those weapons had the potential to send destruction upon the island of Rhodes behind him.

The larger ship's deck overfilled with the exiled. They filled every square foot of the old wood planks, and some pressed over the side rails. Many of them held refurnished firearms and aimed upon Samson and his little craft. The bullets began to fly by him. Their weapons were not as accurate as they were when originally manufactured. Some shots began to pierce the hull and punch additional holes in the already damaged sail. A bullet grazed Samson's side and ricocheted off the edge of one of his ribs. Despite the wound, he continued on.

Samson wrapped the rope around the cylinders, but not too tightly. He then pressed the end of the spear of the gun between them and the strands of rope. In a few moments the ship would be just yards from his vessel.

Samson spotted Haden on the deck, and could see that he had also taken notice. Haden appeared to be giving sudden and stern orders to the crew. The ship started to turn away from the intersecting course with Samson's small boat. He reacted quickly and turned the small boat so that he was running in the same direction as the sea wind. At this angle it would be difficult for the larger ship to maneuver around him. He tied off the tiller and boom of the mainsail again with this new aggressive course.

Samson held the spear gun with the explosives fastened to its projectile, and drew the elastic band back so that the weapon was ready to launch. The exiles on board the ship continued to fire. The missing shots released small bursts of water around his boat. The splashes they made were so small that the bullets seemed harmless.

The hull of the larger ship came closer and closer at an angle perpendicular to his boat. If he did not hit the ship of the exiled, it might actually be able to pass directly in front of his bow without even touching his vessel. His only chance was to fire the spear gun with explosives.

Samson held out the lighter and clicked the button to start the flame. The sea breeze was partially negated now that he was traveling with it, but the flame still did not catch easily. He pressed the button again and again, and aimed the flame to the fuse of the explosives. A flame emitted from the long barrel and survived for a few moments. One of the fuse ends in the path of the flame sparked and then caught fire. Soon the other fuses also burned from the original.

Samson pulled the butt of the spear gun against his shoulder and aimed it at the hull of Haden's ship. His boat rocked and the bow rose and fell with each wave. He did his best to estimate a time when his pulling of the trigger would release the spear just above the level of the water and toward the ship. He pulled the trigger, sending the spear out.

The bullets proved there lethalness. One hit Samson in the chest. He lost his strength almost instantly and fell over the side of the boat when the bow was only a few yards from the attacking ship. He knew the shot was fatal.

As he sunk into the water, the world suddenly moved in an abbreviated motion. The sunrays pierced the surface of the water directly above him and separated into billowing ribbons travelling into the depths. The vessels' paths were about to cross directly in front of the light of the sun. The larger ship's bow began to block the sunlight from Samson.

At that moment, the explosives detonated. His fired spear must have found its mark and landed in the fiberglass hull of the exiled. Fragments and fibers of the ship arched out in all directions as the explosives inflicted their damage. The ship above began to sink.

Samson looked down to his body. His legs and arms were entangled in rope. Blood left his body and colored the water with a red dust. His body did not react to his thoughts. He did not close his eyes, and yet the sunrays in the water dimmed. Samson heard the sound of children playing. It sounded like they were playing in the surf.

Made in the USA
· Columbia, SC
30 January 2020